THE LONDON LEAP

SAMANTHA KRAMER

Library of Congress Control Number: 2025901306

ISBN 979-8-9917201-0-6 (paperback edition)

ISBN 979-8-9917201-1-3 (ebook edition)

Book Cover by Darius Kelly

First Edition: March 2025

To every version of myself who dreamed of being a writer and everyone who believed in me along the way.

1

I have no desire to go to London. None at all. I'd never planned to fly across the ocean by myself to begin my freshman year. But here I am. I'd been trying to push this day out of my mind ever since I found out my fate. In the beginning, it was easy. It was still months away. But each day, time continued to tick closer until the day actually arrived. Now, here I am, beginning the future I'd been trying to deny.

As the wheels of my plane screech to a halt on the runway of London's Heathrow Airport, the weight of my new reality crushes down on me. Outside the plane's window, a foreign land greets me. Beyond the concrete of the airport runway, I don't know what to expect.

I rub my eyes as I wait in line to exit the plane. I don't know what time it is, but it doesn't matter; I'm in severe need of a nap. Trying to sleep on the plane had been absolutely brutal. I'd consider myself lucky if I managed to get two hours of sleep.

Once I'm free from the plane, I'm on my own to navigate through the bustling terminal full of unfamiliar faces. My heart pounds in rhythm to the rush of people around me as I find the baggage carousel. I pinch myself, hoping I'll wake up in a dorm room at Boston Southeast University, the school I should've been going to, instead of getting ready to start a year at London City University all alone.

I text my dad first that I landed safely, then send a message to my best friend Emily. My phone immediately vibrates in my hand and displays Emily's contact picture.

I answer immediately. "Emily," I exclaim. "I thought you'd get charged if you called internationally."

"I'll keep it short," she says. "I just wanted to wish you luck. You're going to kill it, Olivia. Have the most amazing adventure. Call me once you get settled in."

"I'm going to miss you so much," I remind her. "Don't have too much fun without me."

Emily should be the one here in London instead of me. She always embraced change and could make a decision without looking back. In sixth grade, I remember she'd proudly declared to me in between class changes that she'd decided she wanted to cut her long hair to her shoulders.

Don't you want to think about it? I'd asked her. Emily loved her long hair, always curling or braiding it. It was part of her style.

It'd been a silly question to ask. Once Emily made up her mind, she stuck with it. *We're in middle school now,* she'd said. *I'm ready for a change.*

The next day, she arrived at school with a fresh haircut.

Then, in eighth grade, when Emily's family was about to move to a new house in their neighborhood, I sobbed on the floor of her empty bedroom. We'd spent so many sleepovers there, her mom making waffles in the morning in their robin's-egg blue kitchen. Even though her new house was only one street away, it just wouldn't be the same.

But Emily never cried. She packed up her room without a hint of emotion. *It has to happen,* she'd said. Her parents had been wanting a bigger house so they could have a guest room for extended family to visit. When they'd found one in the same neighborhood that checked all their boxes, they'd jumped on it. I think I was more upset than anyone in her family.

If Emily was in London, beginning her freshman year of college, she'd go into it strong and confident. But instead, she was at Boston Southeast University with our other best friend, Ryan, and her new roommate, Maddie.

It'd always been the plan to go to BSU and be roommates. To have the college experience together. Emily, Ryan, and I had opened our letters from BSU together one afternoon in March. While they'd celebrated their acceptance, my heart had sunk into the pit of my stomach.

Dear Olivia,

Congratulations! Because of your outstanding academic performance, we invite you to complete your freshman year at our partner university, London City University, through our year-abroad scholarship program. This exciting opportunity will provide you with a unique cultural experience, while also completing necessary Boston Southeast University courses alongside other scholarship students. Should you continue to demonstrate excellent academic performance, you'll be able to seamlessly transfer into BSU for the next academic year in your intended major of architecture.

Our year-abroad program includes a scholarship for room and board, as well as major-specific classes in London that will set you ahead and give you a worldly approach to your studies. We hope you will take advantage of this opportunity for the upcoming academic year.

I hadn't applied anywhere else because I knew getting into BSU was a given. I'd worked extra hard to maintain my grades and build my resume by getting involved in student government. I had everything BSU admissions would want. But my plan had worked a little too well. When my dad saw that I'd be offered a scholarship, there was no question about it—I had to take it. Now, I have no other choice than to spend my freshman year in London, where I'd be held captive until I could come home for Christmas break.

Here's how things were supposed to have gone: I'd work really hard and get accepted into BSU with a scholarship that was offered on their campus in Boston. I'd be roommates with Emily for all four years, and we'd make new friends together. I'd study architecture, get my master's, then move back to Bartonsville, my hometown, and work as a historical preservation architect. I had it all figured out.

Only now, a year abroad meant that my best friends and I wouldn't be together. I wouldn't be in Boston with my family only an hour away in Bartonsville. I wouldn't be able to come home on the weekends.

I wouldn't be moving into Crescent Hall in Boston with Emily. With the plan out the window, Emily immediately started looking for a new roommate. When she found Maddie, they'd instantly bonded over their shared love of caramel lattes, pop music, and collecting succulent plants. Emily couldn't stop bubbling with excitement and saying that it seemed like she and Maddie were like the exact same person.

I, on the other hand, wouldn't find out about my living situation until I arrived. And even then, my dad wouldn't be there to help me tack up a bulletin board when I couldn't reach the right spot. My sister Charlotte wouldn't get to help me decorate like we'd talked about. And my brother Lucas wouldn't be there to complain that we were overthinking the whole decorating process.

I can't believe I'm getting emotional about not hearing Lucas complain, I grumble as I watch for my suitcase on the conveyor belt.

Finally, my overstuffed, black suitcase glides by. The ugly thing had been staring me down in the corner of my bedroom, an awful reminder of the future I didn't want. I grip the handle of the bag and tug with all my strength until I have it upright and free from the carousel. Once my arm workout is out of the way, I make my way to the passenger pick-up area and find the representative, a woman with a tight ponytail and wide-leg pants, holding a sign that reads, BSU ABROAD STUDENTS.

"We're waiting on one more student," she crisply informs me. "Then we'll be on our way to orientation."

Next to me, a man in a business suit is reuniting with his wife and two children. They all hug each other, and I have to look away so I don't start crying in front of my new classmates.

Once everyone has arrived, we pile into a big, black bus for orientation. Jet lag finally catches up with me, and before I know it, I'm jolted awake when the bus stops in front of London City University's main academic building. The three-story brick building sits pleasantly on a short street of identical buildings with blue doors. A double-decker bus zips by on the adjacent street. The buzz of the city is nearby, but on this street, the world seems to sit still.

I follow the representative into a large lecture hall. I hope this doesn't take too long. At least I'm not alone now; we're all BSU scholarship students here.

"Hey," a girl with black hair and blue streaks says. She slides into the seat next to me. "I'm so excited about being in London. I can't wait to get out and explore. I mean, this is incredible!"

I shrug. "Sure is."

"I'm Chloe," she says.

"Olivia."

"So nice to meet you," Chloe says. "I'm sure we'll see each other a lot in the dorm and all."

Our orientation leader, a peppy brunette named Laura, gets our attention and begins our orientation. My head spins with all the information Laura fires at us, along with trying to keep up with her accent when she talks fast. *Never leave your belongings out of sight. You'll need an Oyster Card for the Tube, London's public transport. Here's a list of common British phrases. Stand to the right on escalators. Don't lose your student ID card.*

"Alright," Laura says. "The first-year residence halls are right down the road. Once you pick up your ID card from me, you'll be good to go and ready to get moved in."

I join the line, or queue as I've just learned it's called over here, of students. Soon, I'll be able to get settled into my dorm, call Emily, and finally let my body have a long, uninterrupted nap.

"Name, please?" Laura says when I reach the front of the line.

"Olivia McAlister," I answer. A yawn escapes. Thank goodness the dorm's close by.

Laura scans her clipboard. "Ah, that's you," she says.

"So, good news and bad news. The university accepted more first-year students this year, so there's not enough space in the first-year residence halls. You're one of the lucky ones who'll have a single room in the second-year residence hall, Queen Victoria House. It's quite lovely, and…"

She keeps talking, but I don't hear what she says. My mouth simply hangs open. This could not be happening. No way was I going to a dorm away from all the other BSU students. The second-years probably all knew each other. And if they were second-years, they definitely weren't here against their will.

"Here's your ID card, Olivia," Laura says, breaking me from my thoughts. "The cab will be waiting for you out front."

I didn't hear where she said Queen Victoria House was, but I'm guessing it's not near the first-year residence hall if I'm being shuttled away in the cab. So much for seeing Chloe around the dorms. The driver helps load my suitcase into the car.

"Where, exactly, are we going?" I ask him.

"North London," he answers in a gruff accent, providing another reminder that I'm in this new, unfamiliar place. "We've got about a thirty-minute ride."

I groan as I climb into the back seat of the cab. I remember Laura mentioning that, like the name suggests, London City University's campus is spread out all over the city, with dorms and academic buildings dotted about. I rest my head against the window and watch as the hustle and bustle of downtown London is soon replaced by a wealthy residential area.

"This is it," my driver says. He pulls my suitcase out for me then points to a private driveway. "You'll find the residence hall up at the top of the drive."

My suitcase drags and thumps behind me on the paved drive. Each step I take seems like one step farther away from home and a step closer to the unknown. I make my way up the dorm's steep driveway and am greeted by a brick building sprawled out across a fresh green lawn. Windows are ajar, giving me a glimpse into some of the already decorated rooms. I'm definitely the last one moving in.

Well, here goes nothing.

I scan my student card at Queen Victoria's towering black door.

"Good afternoon," a blond boy at the front desk greets me in a pleasant British accent. "You must be the new first-year."

"That's me." The new first-year. Probably the only new first-year here.

"You're really lucky to be given a room in the second-year hall," the boy says with a touch of sincerity. "I'm serious. QVH is so much nicer than where the first-years live."

"Okay," I say for lack of better words. I didn't care how bad the first-year dorms were; it would've been a thousand times better to be surrounded by other students who were just as clueless about London.

Exhaustion tugs at me, and I fight back a yawn. I don't want to make a bad impression, but my social battery is practically empty after my flight and orientation. I honestly don't know how I've managed to stay awake for this long.

"Let me help you to your room. I'm Gabriel. I'm here at the front desk most days when I'm not in class. Happy to provide assistance or answer any questions you may have."

So, he was a student here as well. I guess like the resident assistant of the building. Maybe Gabriel could be my friend. I'm pretty sure that's one of the duties of an RA.

Gabriel walks me down to my room, which is on the first floor, thank goodness. The building's old and doesn't have any elevators, so I can't imagine trying to drag my suitcase up multiple flights of stairs. I scan my student ID card, which also functions as my room key, then I'm on my own for real.

My dorm room sits there, white and bare, waiting for me to bring life into it. The bed, closet, and desk are all squeezed into the shoebox of space. I could work with the empty room if only I could've brought another suitcase full of decorations.

My bedroom at home overflows with color. I have an entire shelf that houses my acrylic paints and a corner devoted to painting. My project last year was collecting scrapbook paper squares and paint chips to make a mismatched, colorful mural behind my desk. String lights and paper ivy from the craft store hang down behind my rainbow-colored quilt. I can't think of a single color that isn't present in my room.

But I didn't have enough space in my suitcase to bring anything more than a garland of fake white flowers. It'd already been a struggle to get my suitcase zipped closed once all my clothes and essentials were packed, and even that was pushing the weight limit. My dad told me I could buy anything else I wanted over in England, like string lights or a colorful duvet cover.

I rip open a pack of thumbtacks I'd packed and hang the garland above my bed. And I'm done. I place my suitcase on the floor. I can do this. I can unpack my clothes. I can try to make this tiny room feel a little like home.

Home. I miss Bartonsville so much. I miss my family and my best friend. My best friend. Emily. I'd told her I'd call once I got to my dorm.

Immediately, Emily's familiar shoulder-length brown hair and freckles fill my screen. It feels like it's been a lifetime since I've seen her face.

"Olivia," she says. "Yay, you made it! How is it?"

"I don't know. I haven't gotten to go out and do anything yet. I'm so jet-lagged," I say. I can't help but yawn. "I don't even know what time it is anymore."

"I'm so jealous," Emily says. "You'll have to send me pictures and tell me about all the fun stuff you do." Emily flips the camera to show me Ryan and her roommate sitting on her dorm room's futon. "We're sorting through our outfits for sorority recruitment tomorrow. Ryan's not being much help at all," she says with a groan.

"You're rushing?" I ask. Sororities were never a part of our college plan. Emily had always talked about joining a club soccer team, and I'd wanted to get involved with student government. Then, we were going to join the community service organization together. We'd agreed that we wouldn't have the time or energy for a sorority.

"I am," she says. "Maddie wants to, and I thought it'd be a good way to meet more people. So, I'll let you know how it goes. But I wish you were here with us."

"Me too," I say. I'd give anything to hop on the next departing flight and join my friends in Emily's dorm room.

"Hey, Olivia," Ryan shouts. "Miss you!"

Even from miles away and on my phone's small screen, butterflies fill my stomach. Ryan's dark hair and perfect smile are enough to make me lose the ability to think straight.

"I miss you so much," I say.

Emily flips the camera back on herself.

"London's better than Boston, I bet," Emily assures me. "Gotta go, bye!"

I kick my suitcase aside. I should unpack and try to organize my life, but I want nothing more than a warm shower and a bed. I don't even care that it's still light outside. Right now, I'm in my own nonexistent time zone. Classes start tomorrow, and I have to at least have enough energy in me to try to make some temporary friends. I know this London life isn't going to be forever. I just have to survive these two semesters abroad. Then I get to go back to Boston, where I can be at my dream school with my best friends.

I step into the hallway and make sure I have my key. The nice thing about Queen Victoria House is that there are individual, full bathrooms scattered throughout the hall. Having shared hall baths was one thing I'd been dreading about college, so at least that's one plus to this whole situation. My dad had given me a travel-sized shampoo and body wash so I could at least put off trying to find a grocery store for a few days.

"Hello!" Gabriel's voice catches me off guard. "Are you adjusting alright?"

"I'm just really tired," I say. Which isn't completely a lie because I'm exhausted.

"If you need anything at all, my room's the first one on the hall," Gabriel says, gesturing to his door. "That's what I'm here for."

Standing in the hallway, the realization finally hits me: there's no one here who knows anything about me. I nod while I hold back tears. I refuse to cry in front of anyone here, especially not my RA, who probably could already tell that I was a bit upset. "Thanks," I manage to get out.

"Of course," Gabriel says as he scans his key on his door. "If I don't see you tomorrow, hope you have a great first day. Don't hesitate to let me know if there's anything I can do to help."

Once I'm behind the locked door of the bathroom, the silence envelopes me. I feel like I'm a rubber band, being stretched out as far as it can go until it finally snaps.

I'm completely on my own now. There's no Emily and Ryan here to confide in. My dad's bedroom isn't right down the hall. When I think about the massive ocean that separates me from all the people I love, I can't seem to breathe anymore. And right on cue, the tears break free. At first, it's only one, but once it rolls down my cheek, the floodgates let loose. I'm stuck here, with no escape, until Christmas break. All I have is myself, which is my darkest nightmare come true.

MY ALARM SCREAMS AT ME AND I FORCE MY EYES OPEN. White walls. White closet. White floor. Four tacks holding up my pathetic garland. Nope, not a dream. I'm still in Queen Victoria House. My head pounds from jet lag, as well as the fact that I didn't eat dinner last night. I got plenty of sleep, but I stumble out of bed in a fog. My suitcase glares at me from the corner of the room, begging me to unpack it. I should've dealt with that yesterday.

I pull out the first thing I can find, a black tank top and jeans. It won't matter what I wear because I'm going to stick out like a sore thumb as soon as I step out of my room. I'm going to be that new girl. That new American girl. That first-year in a second-year dorm where everyone already knows each other.

I glance in my mirror and add a gold necklace and my velvet, lavender headband for a pop of color. I can't go out in full neutral colors, especially since my dark brown hair and brown eyes aren't much help in this situation.

I'm a firm believer in making everything as colorful as possible. What's the point of being boring? It might be because I'm an artist, but I've always wanted to find the right colors that fit every moment. Black fits my mood about being at this school, but hopefully, the lavender would be the touch of good luck I'd need for today. I double-check that I have my student card, a notebook, and a pen in my backpack, then take a deep breath and step out into the hallway.

Here goes nothing, my first day of college in a foreign country.

I'm clueless about where the dining hall is because, of course, in orientation, they'd only mentioned where the dining hall closest to the first-year dorm was.

I peek down the hall, but the front desk sits abandoned. I don't want to disturb Gabriel, but he did say he was here if I needed anything. The first door on the hall near the front desk displays his handwritten name on a neon-yellow star cutout, confirming that it's his room.

I lift my fist to knock but catch myself. Not everyone in college is on the exact same schedule as me. He could still be sleeping and not have to be anywhere until hours later. There's no one coming from either end of the hall and I'm all alone, so I crouch down on the floor, then lie on my side. The cool hardwood floor presses against my cheek, and I try to ignore the specks of dirt that are now visible. The crack under his door is pitch black. Fantastic.

A door creaks open, and footsteps echo through the floorboards. I sit up, but I'm not quick enough.

"Are you okay?" An American accent.

I scramble to pick myself up off the floor to face the girl staring at me. She's short, almost mouse-like, but she stands with her chin tilted up making her seem as if she's towering over me. She has a blue-patterned dress on, and her long blonde hair falls in loose, natural waves.

"Yeah, I'm fine," I say, brushing dirt off my jeans. *Oh my god, so embarrassing. She totally saw me lying on the floor.*

"Gabriel doesn't start class until around ten. In case you were looking for him," she says.

I want to run back into my room and never leave for the rest of the year.

"Are you the new American fresher who's living here this year?" the girl asks.

I nod. It really can't be less obvious that I don't fit in here. And I've already given one of my neighbors a less-than-perfect first impression.

"I'm Bailey," she says. "Gabriel sent out an email about you last night and I was hoping to run into you. Gabriel was saying you're in the scholarship program through Boston Southeast. I did that last year too."

So now everyone in Queen Victoria House knows about me and knows I'm not meant to be here. At least Bailey had gone through the same situation as me last year. Maybe she'd have more sympathy for me.

"But you're a second year?"

"I am. I loved London so much I decided to stay here

and finish out school. Maybe the city will have that effect on you too." She gives me a genuine smile, and my embarrassment evaporates a little.

"I don't know, I really want to be in Boston. It's where my best friends are. And Boston Southeast was my dream school."

"Suit yourself," Bailey says. "But make sure you enjoy your time here. I wasted my whole first month here last year complaining about how much I missed home when really London became the place for me."

My stomach roars, a reminder that I'm going to have to figure out where the nearest dining hall or grocery store is sooner rather than later. "I'm going to, uh, I guess, head to that coffee shop down the road and get a muffin before class." At least I knew what to expect at a coffee chain. Was it my first choice? No, but it would work for today.

Bailey shakes her head. "Cafeteria's going to be much better, trust me. I'll take you there, and you can sit with me and meet some of my friends. We'll help you get to class and get adjusted. I know it's all a bit overwhelming."

London City's North cafeteria is a short walk from Queen Victoria House. Bailey pushes open the glass door, and immediately, it's like I've walked into a bakery. Already I'm glad I'm here instead of a chain coffee shop. Bailey points out the three different food stations and explains what they usually serve. I get a warm chocolate croissant and a bowl of vanilla Greek yogurt with honey, granola, and blueberries, then follow Bailey to her usual spot, a wooden table near a window.

"Bailey!" A British, ginger-haired girl jumps out of her seat and hugs Bailey. Her long, auburn hair practically comes down to her waist, and her face is framed with gold hoops. Her fingers are filled with mismatched gold and silver rings, and stacks of matching bracelets line her wrists. "Oh my god, I missed you over the summer. How was your flight? How was California?"

I set my tray down beside Bailey, then take a bite of my croissant and pretend to be really invested in my food while she catches up with her friend.

"I'm Hannah," the ginger girl finally says. "Bailey says you're a fresher. How exciting!"

"Yeah," I say. I give her a smile. This is a good start. Maybe Hannah and Bailey can be my temporary friends.

Hannah turns her attention back to Bailey. "Ronan said he was going to come sit with us. So maybe Finn will too."

"Hey Hannah, Bailey!" A loud boy comes bouncing over to our table with a bowl of porridge and slips into the seat next to Hannah. He must be Ronan. His tight, black curls stick out in every direction, but it works for him.

"Finn's coming," Ronan says. "I think. You never know with him. Hey Hannah, can I steal that strawberry?" Ronan reaches for the last strawberry on Hannah's plate, but she pushes away his hand.

"Nooo, it's mine." She waves it in his face before taking a bite.

"Aw, come on. This is how you're going to treat me on the first day of class?"

A few minutes later, another boy slips into the seat across from Ronan. He runs a hand through his honey-colored curls, then adjusts his tortoiseshell glasses. He has nothing except a cup of coffee.

"Good morning, everyone," he deadpans.

"Finn," Ronan says, ignoring his tone. "What took you so long?"

"I overslept. Not the best way to start the semester, I suppose," Finn says. He digs into his tan backpack, pulls out a paperback book, and cracks it open.

Ronan nudges the book up to read the cover. "*Frankenstein*?" Ronan says. "Seriously, mate, what's that all about?"

Finn offers Ronan a shrug in response.

"Finley Abbott is the smartest one in our year," Ronan says and claps his hands. "Always reading or studying for something."

Finn ignores Ronan's comment, and I can't tell if Ronan's being serious or sarcastic.

Ronan points to me. "Sorry, I didn't catch your name?"

"I'm Olivia. I'm new here." Obviously.

"That's great," Ronan says. "Finn, Olivia. Olivia, Finn."

Finn's eyes remain glued to his page. He makes no

effort to indicate that he heard Ronan, but at least Ronan made an effort to introduce me.

The group launches into a conversation about their summers. Everyone except me and Finn. Finn's too busy ignoring us all, so I don't know why he even came to sit with us. Bailey and Hannah seem nice so far, but they'd also known each other for a whole year and were definitely close.

Once again, my thoughts drift back to my friends. I should be sitting in a dining hall in Boston, laughing with Emily and Ryan about our own inside jokes, like the man we'd always see at the town diner eating cherry ice cream. We should be making new friends together who'll be our forever college friends. Instead, I'm having to make friends with people who I'd only have for a year, then I'd move back to Boston and never see them again.

"What's your first class?" Bailey asks, finally turning to talk to me. "We'll have to get going soon, but I'll help you get to the Tube and make sure you get to the right station."

I pull out the printed schedule I was given yesterday during orientation. I make quick work to try to memorize my class locations within the next ten seconds so I don't stand out as a first-year walking around with my schedule. Not that I won't already stand out, but anything to help my case at this point is worth trying.

"It's London's Walking History," I say. A general education history class that all first-years are required to take. Something about learning about the city you're living in. An easy history class that should be no problem. At least, I remember them mentioning that during orientation.

Finn makes eye contact with me for the first time and scowls before returning to his book. I'm not sure what any of us did to upset him.

"That class was my favorite. It's so fun, it doesn't even feel like a class," Bailey says. "You learn so much cool stuff about London. Then you get to go out and see it. It'll really help you get to know the city."

After we wrap up breakfast, Bailey walks with me to the nearest Tube station. She has a class in a different building, but we'll at least get to commute together. In my orientation packet, they gave us a map of the Tube lines, but all the different colors and cross sections made my head spin. I don't know how I'd ever learn my way around without having to consult a map.

"Okay, so you'll just take the Northern line down to Tottenham Court Road. You won't have to change lines at all," Bailey says as we enter the station. "Then, walk like seven minutes and you'll see the first-year building on your right. It's a super easy walk and right in the city."

Everyone else around me scans their Oyster cards without even thinking. When it's my turn, I tap my card and follow Bailey down the long flight of stairs. Thank goodness I can follow her. Northern to Tottenham Court, then walk. I repeat the directions constantly in my head until it becomes the beat that I'm walking to. Northern, Tottenham, walk.

A train slows to a stop in front of our platform, and Bailey and I join the crowd of morning commuters. It's as if every single person in London has decided they want to get on this exact train at this exact moment. I'm absorbed in the mass of people and lose sight of Bailey. I try to push my way closer to the train. But I'm too late.

The doors of the train close, and only then do I see Bailey. We make eye contact, her from the window inside the train and me, standing on the platform with everyone else who's still waiting. Bailey's jaw drops, and I can feel mine mirroring hers. Then the train whisks her off.

This can't be happening.

So much for Bailey helping me get to class. I glance at the time on my phone. I'm still on schedule at least, but I have absolutely no idea where I'm going. I don't know if the next train is going to the same stop I need. I would assume so because that makes sense. I think. I don't remember what they said about the Tube in orientation. I type out a text to Bailey begging for directions, but it doesn't go through.

Lovely.

In just a few minutes the next train is already arriving. I'm closer this time, and of course, with my luck, it's super easy to get on the train now that Bailey's gone. I chance it and cram myself inside the car with everyone else. I grasp a pole and steady myself as the train takes off.

The silence hovers around us on the train, and I'm afraid even my breathing is too loud. But I don't know where I'm going, and I've never liked not knowing how I'm getting from point A to point B.

"Excuse me," I say in a loud whisper to the man sharing the pole with me. I'm suddenly self-conscious of my American accent and I feel like everyone's looking at me now. I want to take it all back and scream, *Never mind! I'll just figure it out by myself!*

The man in the suit makes eye contact with me, so there's no going back now.

"I lost my friend, and this is my first time on the Tube," I continue in my elevated whisper. "I need to get to Tottenham Court Road. Am I on the right train?"

Suit Man confirms that I am indeed in the right place, going the right direction, and that I'll hear my stop announced soon. I give him a quick thank you and keep my lips zipped until I reach my stop.

About twenty minutes later, I'm free from the Tube. I ride the escalator up in silence until the outdoors greets me. I'm not in the suburbs of north London anymore, but right in the heart of the city. It seems like everyone is out here walking in all different directions.

As soon as I'm above ground, my panicked text to Bailey goes through, and I receive a string of messages from her. She apologized three times within her two texts and gave me extremely detailed directions on how to get to the academic building. I shoot her a text letting her know I made it.

I take off down the street, reading Bailey's directions, until I arrive at the academic building. The signs in the main lobby point me up to the third floor, where First-Year Introduction to London's Walking History is meeting. I climb the three flights of narrow stairs, then barely have time to catch my breath since the door to the classroom is right next to the stairs. *Breathe*, I tell myself, *even if it's hard.* Everyone in here is new to this school too. At least half of them are Americans who probably want to be back in Boston. They're all like me. I can do this. In this class, I'm not alone.

The classroom walls are just wide enough to fit a few scattered tables. There's room for no more than twenty students. So much for this being a big, lecture-style class like I expected. I immediately spot a girl I recognize from orientation.

"Hi," I say. "Can I sit here?"

"Hey," she says and introduces herself as Joanne. "You're in the Boston Southeast program too, right?"

Joanne and I talk as the rest of the class makes their way in. It's good to have someone else to talk to who's as unfamiliar with this city and school as I am. I glance over at the door right as Finley Abbott walks into the classroom. He sits down at a table on the other side of the room, diagonally from me. Just like this morning, he pulls out *Frankenstein* and dives back in. Did Ronan say Finn was a first-year?

No, that wouldn't make sense. Then why's he in this class?

A group of students, engulfed in conversation, come in and sit in the row behind us. Their accents remind me that not every first-year in this class is American. Of course, there are first-year British students who were planning on attending this university for all four years. They came here because this school was their first choice.

"I can't wait to get to know everyone," Joanne says.

I wonder if Emily and Ryan were meeting all kinds of new people in their classes. My heart yearns to have them in this classroom with me. I'd be sitting in between Emily and Ryan, then we'd spend all our free time together. It would've been the perfect opportunity for me and Ryan to grow closer.

Ryan moved two houses down from me in seventh grade and had every single class with Emily, which automatically made him our second best friend. The three of us have been inseparable since middle school. It wasn't until high school, when Ryan grew taller and his voice got deeper, that I became aware that I might've liked him as more than a friend. But I wasn't about to tell him or Emily. I went through high school secretly admiring Ryan and wishing for more.

Emily and I never talked about Ryan as anything more than our best friend. I was scared to know if she ever spent nights lying awake in bed wondering what Ryan was doing or dreaming of kissing him in the rain. I'd always told myself that when we got to college, I'd finally admit to Ryan and Emily how I felt. But then I had to go to London, and now Emily has Ryan all to herself. They have every opportunity to fall in love. Or Ryan might meet someone else. He might find someone who's prettier or funnier than me.

I should've told Ryan I loved him before I went to the airport. I almost did. Even though Emily and Ryan moved into their dorms a week before I left, Ryan had made the trip home to help send me off. He said he was coming home for the day to watch his sister's gymnastics competition, but I found it awfully convenient that he had the time to help me load my suitcase in my dad's blue SUV before we headed to the airport.

"Alright! Our adventurer is off to have the best freshman year," he'd said, then pulled me in for a hug.

"Ryan?" I said as I looked into his eyes. They were like a storm cloud, blue-gray and staring right back at me. It was my chance. *I've loved you since tenth grade, but I was too afraid to say anything because what if you loved Emily instead of me? Or what if Emily loved you? Or what if that ruined our friendship? Anyway, I really love you and…*

"I'll miss you," were the only words I could find.

And that was it. I spent the whole flight wishing I could go back to that moment and change things. I'd had my chance, and now it was gone. I mean, I'd be home in December for Christmas, but who knows what things would be like.

Our professor walks in, which snaps me out of my daydream. He can't be any older than his mid-thirties and insists we call him Mike instead of Dr. Richards. For some reason, I pictured British professors dressing in full-on suits, but Mike's wearing a Superman T-shirt and shorts.

He passes out our syllabus and runs through the dates of essays and projects and how we can get in touch with him if we have any questions.

"So," Mike says. "This class is called London's Walking History, which, as the name suggests, means we'll be walking. I'll assign everyone a partner who you'll be working with. You'll have a list of historical clues, which will help to lead you to the site you're looking for. That, and paying attention to my lectures. When you find a site on the list, take a picture of it. At the end of the term, you and your partner will turn in your pictures and a group write-up about your process of going about London."

Mike passes out our lists and my eyes about pop out of their sockets. One hundred places to find? The clues make zero sense, like: *Green and yellow meet blue at her very own stop.* I'm sorry, but what? How was I supposed to figure out what these clues were even asking while out in a city I knew nothing about?

I let out a sigh and Joanne gives me a sympathetic smile.

"It'll be fun," she whispers. "It's like a scavenger hunt."

Easy for her to say. She'd told me how excited she was to be in London and that she was hoping to get a spot in the scholarship program. Lucky her. I had no interest in exploring London beyond my dorm and class buildings.

Mike begins to call the names of partners, and I hope I get paired up with someone else who's in the Boston

Southeast program. At least that way, I could get to know someone who will be transferring back to Boston at the end of the year. And it could be a built-in friend.

"Joanne Smith and Alyssa Rodgerson. Olivia McAlister and Finley Abbott…"

My heart sinks. I glance over and see Finn still has his book out, though he's moved it under his desk. What is his problem?

"Right then, everyone, go ahead and find your partners, introduce yourselves, and make an action plan for finding these sites. We'll start our first official lecture tomorrow," Mike says.

Finn picks up his backpack and clutches his paperback. He makes his way over to my table, his tall frame hovering above me.

"Are you Olivia?" he says without a hint of emotion in his voice.

"That's me," I say. I want to call him out about our earlier introduction. He knows who I am. But I don't want to make a poor impression if he's the one I'm going to be stuck working with for the rest of the year.

Finn nods and takes the seat Joanne had been sitting in. His dark blond hair rests on his head in perfect curls, his round tortoise glasses accent his hazel eyes, and he's wearing khakis and a black shirt. I can't help thinking about what Ryan might wear to class. He would probably dress pretty casually in just a T-shirt and sweatpants. Not that the difference in clothes mattered; when it came down to it, Ryan was just a better person. Ryan would never sit through class reading and ignoring the professor.

"Okay. So," I say. "This assignment looks pretty overwhelming." Finn's face is blank. Maybe I shouldn't have said that, and I worry he's now going to think I'm some stupid American first-year. I can't let him believe that stereotype.

"I'm from Bartonsville. It's near Boston. In Massachusetts. In America," I say to try to clear things up. "I'm not from here. I don't know the city very well."

Finn blinks. "You could have stopped with Boston. I know basic geography."

Way to confirm even more so that I'm a stupid American!

"Of course. Anyway…for these clues, I'll have to do some research because, obviously, I'm pretty clueless about London," I say.

Finn adjusts his glasses and moves his sheet in between us. He points to the first clue. "Number one is Parliament, two is Big Ben, three's Westminster Abbey, four's the statue of Winston Churchill. Shall I go on?" He raises an eyebrow and looks me directly in the eyes without an ounce of emotion on his face.

I stiffen in my chair. "I mean, I don't mind doing my end of the research to find some of the answers."

How did he even know the answers so quickly if he wasn't even paying attention? He didn't need to flaunt his knowledge right in my face.

"Don't bother," Finn says. "I know them all. Here's the plan." Finn runs his hand through his hair. "I'll tell you the answers. We'll go to all the sites and knock them out, then we're done."

Thanks to my lovely first impression, he most definitely thinks I'm an idiot who can't be trusted with this assignment. Even though I don't want to be in London, it doesn't mean I can't complete good, quality schoolwork.

"I don't want you to just give me the answers," I say. "You're not even giving me a chance to figure out some things on my own. I want to at least try."

Finn gives me a careless, one-shoulder shrug. "I just want to get this done the quickest way possible. We're not making this project last all term."

"Alright then, everyone, that's it for the first day," Mike says, interrupting any response I could've made to Finn. "I look forward to getting to know everyone."

Yeah, it's pretty clear my partner couldn't care less about getting to know me. Finn starts to pack up right as Mike walks over to our table and taps his hand in front of where Finn's sitting.

"Finn, would you stay back for a minute so I can talk to you after class?" Mike says.

Finn drops his backpack beside his chair, and his whole body deflates. He doesn't even meet Mike's eyes. "Absolutely."

I bet Mike heard how rude Finn was being to me. Or he saw him reading in class. Or maybe Mike's going to make him do the project all on his own since he acted like such a know-it-all. That would serve him right. Then Mike could let me be in a group of three with Joanne and

Alyssa, and I'd have friends in my actual program. Friends I could actually keep all through college.

All would be right in the world.

As right as things could be for a London history class I didn't want to take at a college I didn't want to attend.

I pack up my stuff while Finn sits unmoving next to me. I offer him a small smile as a goodbye, but he looks away and suddenly becomes fascinated by the detail on the table. Alright, then. My walking history class was off to a fantastic start.

3

"Finley Abbott is the biggest jerk I've ever met," I say to Bailey and Hannah at dinner. Bailey had texted me that afternoon (with another apology included), inviting me to join them in the evening. "He doesn't pay attention, and he probably thinks I'm an idiot after how things went in class today. And why was he so rude this morning?"

Bailey twirls some spaghetti around her fork. "That's just how Finn is. He's always been quiet."

"I don't know how we're going to get this project done if he's going to act like he doesn't want to work together," I say.

"I wonder why he's even in that class," Hannah says. She pours some dressing on her salad, then starts mixing it. "It's only for first-years, and he totally took it last year."

Bailey wiggles her eyebrows. "Why don't you ask Ronan and get back to us?"

"Stop," Hannah says as her ring-covered hands fly to

her face in an attempt to cover the blush spreading across her cheeks.

"I just don't understand what Finn's deal is," I say. I stab one of my roasted potatoes with my fork and take a bite. I swear, this school must have professional chefs. When I toured BSU, the dining hall had looked like a fun place to hang out with my friends, but I was less than thrilled when I saw the options for lunch; that day, it'd consisted of pizza, French fries, some slimy-looking chicken, and a sad salad bar with wilted lettuce. Maybe it'd been because it was a weekend. I make a mental note to ask Emily and Ryan if it was any better the next time I talked to them.

"I don't know," Bailey says. "Ronan and Finn's rooms were right next to each other last year, so they're good friends. Once Hannah got to know Ronan more, Finn started hanging out with us too. He never really said much. He was in Los Angeles this summer for an internship, so I hung out with him a little over break. I felt bad for him, coming over to LA and not knowing anyone. I still don't feel like I really got to know him any better, though."

"So, does he always read and ignore people?" I ask.

Hannah nods. "Pretty much. Ronan said he spent every minute studying last year. But he's super smart. He got some sort of departmental award at the end of last year for being the most promising first-year physics student."

Hannah twists a stack of rings on her index finger.

"Speaking of Ronan, he texted me after class today and said something about getting drinks at the end of the week to celebrate the start of the school year. Don't you think that's a good sign?"

"Is that even a question?" Bailey says. "Of course! It's so obvious he's into you."

Hannah tries to hide a smile and shields her face with her fingers again. "I don't know," she says. "That's his personality. He's flirty around everyone, so it's hard to tell."

Ryan had a similar kind of personality. He could make anyone feel like they were the center of the universe when they talked to him. And even though Emily and I were his best friends, he would always leave every event we went to with at least two new phone numbers in his phone. One time, after getting an ice cream cone, Ryan left with plans to go fishing with a retired Vietnam War veteran.

So when Ryan and I went to the movies one time, just the two of us, I felt on top of the world. We'd gone to see a new rom-com that Emily and I had been dying to see on the day it came out. But when Emily came down with the flu, Ryan volunteered to go with me. And even though at one point he fell asleep, he still told me he loved it.

Then there was the time when we both had a huge science exam the following day; Ryan had driven to my house with two coffees and his jam-packed science binder. We'd stayed up until two in the morning, half studying, half giggling about nonsense once the caffeine had hit us.

When it was just me and Ryan, it was like I was the only one who mattered. But he'd done the same thing for Emily when they had their AP US History exam. And he'd had such a good time fishing with the veteran that they'd made it a monthly outing.

With Ryan, I knew I was important to him, but so was everyone else. He was always there for me when I needed him, but never specifically asked me to do anything with him one-on-one.

"I think that's a good sign," I say to Hannah. "You should definitely go get drinks with Ronan."

———

After dinner, I'm grateful I have Hannah and Bailey to follow back to the dorm since everything still feels like a blur. There's no way I would've been able to find my way back on my own. The rows of connected brick houses are identical on every street, and I still don't remember which street has the pathway to Queen Victoria House's private drive.

"Hello," Gabriel greets as he's gathering up his stuff at the front desk. Hannah and Bailey call out their hellos, then head to their rooms. But I linger. "How was your day?" Gabriel asks. "Did everything go okay? I was hoping I'd get to see you at some point."

"It's been quite the day," I say, then tell him all about my first Tube experience.

"Well, after that, I think it's safe to say you can handle

anything London throws your way now," he says after I finish my dramatic retelling of the event.

He did have a point. Even though I still didn't know my way around London or how to navigate the Tube, getting to class tomorrow would definitely be easier.

"Besides that, though, I think you're already off to a great start. Hannah and Bailey are wonderful people. It took me a solid semester to even make one friend."

Maybe Gabriel's right. I am off to a decent enough start. My professor for my English class seemed really nice, and my communications professor even brought in some homemade cookies. The only downsides were not being with my real friends and having a terrible partner who wasn't even a first-year. Other than that, I was doing great.

He slings his backpack over his shoulder. "Remember, I'm always here if you need anything or a friend to talk to. I mean it."

As he walks away, I officially decide that everyone I've met so far is genuinely nice. Except for Finn. He's the one exception.

I unlock my door and decide to tackle the task of getting my life together. It feels good to finally unpack my suitcase and get everything organized. I'm not a neat freak or anything, but I like everything to have somewhere it belongs.

Once my clothes are put away, my room's finished. Though it still looks just as drab and boring as it did when I first arrived. I'm jealous of Emily and her decorations, the tapestry, string lights, and posters of her favorite paintings from the MoMA I'd helped pick out. Maybe I'd acquire something here I could use to temporarily decorate my room. Or I could actually paint something.

My fingers itch to paint, to unwind after a particularly long and stressful day. I've always felt there was something about painting that was calming—each careful stroke of the brush, then watching every detail come into play for the final piece.

Of course there hadn't been enough room in my suitcase to bring any of my art supplies either, which meant a calming painting session wouldn't happen again until I went home for Christmas break.

That's one good thing about London, though. It's a big city, bound to have an art store and a bunch of art museums. But it's not like I'm going to go out and buy another easel or order an expensive swivel stool like I had at home. Even once I buy some paint and canvases and brushes, it won't be the same.

At home, canvases of abstract paintings with the brightest colors crowd my bedroom. And my painting corner's a mess, but it's *my* organized mess. There's something about the clutter of dirty brushes and scrap paper stained with faded paint that always makes me feel at ease.

Aside from painting, if there's anything that can fix a hard day or provide ultimate relaxation, it's baking and face masks. I didn't have any of my baking stuff here, or ingredients for that matter, since I still hadn't gone to a grocery store, but I did bring my face mask gel. I pull my long, dark hair up into a bun and take out my cucumber face mask tube. I'll just relax and forget all about Finley Abbott until tomorrow.

I sit on my bed with my face the color of an ogre and flip open my laptop to check my school emails. My phone dings with a new text from Emily, and I breathe a sigh of relief:

Hey! I hope your first day of classes went well. I was thinking about you. Boston is so amazing, and being in a city is wayyyy better than being in Bartonsville. But I bet London is even better. I mean, London's got EVERYTHING. Have you gone sightseeing? Shopping? Gimme all the details. Oh, get this. I've got two classes with Ryan! We've been getting lunch and dinner together, but it's weird without you here. Miss you, love you!

I read her text again, then again, and again. I should be eating every meal with Emily and Ryan. I should be going to class with them and exploring Boston and loving being in the city. I want to pick up my phone and call her, but it's still afternoon there, and she's probably in class.

Outside my dorm, doors slam, and people laugh in the hallways. People I don't know who already know each other. I wait until the laughter subsides before I go across the hall to the water closet, aka bathroom or just toilet as I learned in orientation, to wash off my face. A green face would definitely be the last way I'd want to introduce myself to the other people on my hall.

"Hey!" Hannah calls to me from down the hall. "Love the green."

I pray my green skin hides my now flushed-red skin. *Please don't think I'm weird, please, please.* "Yeah, I was just going to wash it off. It's a cucumber face mask. It's supposed to make your skin clear."

Hannah smiles. "I'm down the road to the store. Want to come and get some groceries?"

"Do they sell cookies?" If I can't make cookies, I'm willing to buy them. I want to eat cookies. I don't even care if they're coconut or oatmeal, my least favorite kinds. All I want is a cookie.

"Of course they do," Hannah says. "Let's go."

———

Forty minutes later I'm sitting on the floor of Bailey's dorm with her, Hannah, a bottle of rosé, and my opened box of chocolate chip cookies. Bailey's room is the exact size of mine with all the same furniture, but I'd never be able to tell that they're the same space. She's traded her white duvet for a mint green one with tiny white polka dots. A woven rug lays in the middle of her hardwood floor, and postcards cover the wall by her desk. She's even made room for a small, cream-colored futon. Everything she owns matches and has a place. I'm surprised I haven't seen pictures of Bailey's room in magazines advertising dorm furniture.

"Wow," I say.

Bailey smiles, obviously taking pride in my astonishment. "Don't worry, it wasn't this put together last year," she says. "Hannah can attest to that. It took me time to get everything and set things up the way I wanted. But it's easier when you're a second-year, and you have a little more of an idea going into decorating. Plus, I had to buy a lot of it over here."

"That's the issue I'm having right now," I say.

"Go to Camden or Shoreditch," Bailey says. "Those areas have all kinds of unique shops. I'll go with you one weekend."

Bailey pops open a bright red record player and fumbles through a case of records beside her desk before settling on one I don't recognize.

"Who's this?" Hannah asks.

"Electric Hinges," Bailey says. "Small band from Essex."

Hannah shakes her head. "Bailey's always discovering these random bands from all over the country. And they're always weird and obscure."

"Electric Hinges is alternative," Bailey says as she pulls down three wine glasses from her desk shelf. "That's not obscure."

Hannah unscrews the wine bottle and starts pouring. "I'm so glad you came to our wine night, Olivia," she says, handing me a glass. "This is our favorite rosé. It's just the store brand so it doesn't cost a fortune, but honestly, it's the best we've tried."

Bailey nods. "And we've tried a lot. Expensive ones too. But this cheap one is my favorite. And it's even better that it doesn't break the bank."

I've never drank before, unless you count the little glasses of champagne my dad would give us on New Year's. In orientation, we learned that the drinking age in England is eighteen. I'd always planned to go out with Emily for our twenty-first birthdays since they were only seven days apart. But when Hannah hands me the wine glass, I take a sip. I didn't see any harm in figuring out what kind of drinks I liked before I went out with Emily.

"Have you talked to Ronan anymore?" I ask Hannah.

Hannah sets down her wine and straightens up. "Yes," she says. "I ran into him in the hall. We had a friendly conversation, you know, but still, he went out of his way to talk to me."

"I think that's really promising," I say. "I'm really good at predicting who'll get together. Senior year of high school I was so certain our classmates Jessica and Henry would get together at prom. No one else believed me, and my friend Ryan even bet me a double-chocolate milkshake they wouldn't. The next day, I was sipping a milkshake, courtesy of Ryan, at the local diner."

"It's just a matter of time before you start dating," Bailey agrees. "Think about Katarina and Scott. Remember how things started with them?"

Hannah drops her shoulders. "But that was Scott. And Katarina's basically a model."

Hannah and Bailey launch into a conversation about more people I've never seen or heard of. My focus shifts to the postcards crowding Bailey's wall, and I study all the different places. If she's a traveler, it's no wonder she decided to stay in London instead of returning to Boston. And it seems like Hannah's her best friend. If Emily and Ryan were here, I'd stay in London too. There'd be no reason not to.

"Did you go to all these places?" I ask, pointing to the collage.

Bailey nods. "That's the perk of living in Europe, being able to jet off for the weekend if you feel like it. I'm going to Greece with Hannah over spring break."

Bailey says it as if it's no big deal, like how everyone at home goes to Cape Cod for spring break.

"Mykonos," Hannah shouts. "I can't wait."

My heart sinks at the thought of spring break. I doubt my dad would pay for a plane ticket to come home for a week. And if Bailey and Hannah are both gone, I don't know what I'll do. I push the thought out of my mind. That was still months away. I'll worry about spring break once I got there.

"Hey," Bailey says. "We're going to get ready to go out to this cool new club in Camden. Want to join us? We're going with a few other guys from QVH."

"That's okay. Thanks for the invite, though." I'm already getting tired, even though it's only nine. I could never make it up to midnight. Emily and Ryan used to get so mad at me when we would try to have movie nights, and I'd fall asleep halfway into the movie because they'd start it too late.

"Next time, then," Hannah says.

I leave Hannah and Bailey to get ready for bed and walk down the hall to my room. A door creaks open, and I can't believe my eyes. Finn walks out of a room two doors down from mine, locking the door behind him. No. Freaking. Way. Finn's on my hall *and* pretty much my neighbor. Hip, hip, hooray.

Maybe he's one of the guys going clubbing with Hannah and Bailey. But when I try to picture Finn in a club, all I can imagine is him standing in a corner frowning. Or reading. He'd be the kind of person to go to the club, then sit in the corner and read and judge everyone else.

"Erm, excuse me," Finn says as he passes me with his head down.

"Hi Finn, nice to see you too," I mumble. He's already down the hall and out the door.

So Finn still despises me and wants nothing to do with me. *Lovely, just lovely.* Class tomorrow is going to be an absolute blast. Although, what if Mike talked to Finn about how rude he was, and that's why he's all mad? Then I'll get a new partner and never have to talk to Finn again. That'd be fantastic.

4

After breakfast the next day, I'm on my own to get to class. Walking History is an everyday class, unlike all our other classes that are every other day. So today, Bailey has to go in the completely opposite direction, but at least I have her to follow to get to the Tube station.

"Do you remember which stop you get off at?" Bailey asks before we part ways.

I nod. "I think so."

"Alright," Bailey says. "I'll see you later. Text me if you get lost. I mean it. But you've totally got this!"

I take a deep breath and stand on the platform alone, waiting for the next train. Finn didn't join us at breakfast this morning, so I don't have him to go to class with, but that's totally fine. I'd rather make the journey on my own than have to sit awkwardly next to him for the commute.

A train arrives, and it's an easy journey to class. I'm

lucky I don't have to change stops. And even though yesterday's journey was a stressful one, Gabriel was right. I do feel a lot more confident on the Tube by myself. Once we arrive at the station, I pull up Bailey's text from yesterday with her walking directions, just in case. The path I took to class yesterday is fading in my memory, and being late to class because I got lost is the last thing I need to happen to me right now.

In class, Mike starts our first official lecture on Westminster and how the United Kingdom government works. It's actually kind of interesting, and Mike does a good job of keeping the class entertained. Well, everyone except Finn. He's slouched in his seat with his long legs stretching out under the table, ready to trip anyone who might walk past him. His book rests in his lap, hidden under his desk, and he's absorbed in whatever it's about. So either Mike didn't talk to him about that, or Finn doesn't care. I wouldn't be surprised if he's being rude to Mike for the sake of being rude.

"Right, so that's the overview of Westminster. You've got the rest of class time to go off to Westminster with your partner and see if you can find some of the sites on your list there," Mike says. "Remember to consider what we talked about in class too."

Next to me, Joanne makes a beeline to Alyssa. They immediately launch into conversation, and, if I didn't know differently, I would've thought they'd known each other for years. That could've been me, but no, I have to drag myself over to Finn. He puts his book away and slings his backpack over his shoulder.

"So, Westminster?" I say.

He doesn't meet my eyes as he explains our plan. "We'll take the Tube and change at Embankment to the Circle or District line. That'll be quickest." He turns to walk out of the classroom, leaving me to trail behind him. *Alright, Mr. Know-It-All. Whatever you say.*

Our building's right near the station so that's one less thing I have to worry about finding. Soon, we're on the Tube headed to Westminster Station. At least Finn knows his way around and how to navigate the Tube. As much as I hate to admit it, I'm thankful that's one less thing I have to worry about.

"Based on the clues, we need to go to Parliament, Big Ben, Westminster Abbey, and the statue of Winston Churchill," Finn says once we're packed into the Tube's car. He sighs and runs his fingers through his hair. "God, this assignment's too easy."

"Why are you even in this class if you're a second-year?" The words slip out of my mouth before I can stop them.

Finn stares straight ahead. "Because I failed it last year, and the university's making me retake it."

So he's going to act like a know-it-all when he failed? Plus, this class seems easy enough. All we have to do is take pictures and figure out all the clues. It'd be a challenge if I was with someone like Joanne, but still. We'd figure it out. Finn's the one who's an idiot if he failed, not me. Serves him right. Of course he's grumpy for being in a class with first-years, but that's his own fault.

The train comes to a stop and we exit at Westminster Station without a word. I follow Finn up the stairs to the cloudy London day.

It seems like the entire city has decided to gather in Westminster today. Or rather every tourist. People with neon-green fanny packs and black sneakers and college T-shirts walk by. A boy sporting a basketball jersey almost steps on my toes as he runs past me to take a picture. An Asian tour group cuts in front of me as the guide babbles something in a language I don't understand. A lady with a selfie stick almost bumps into me, and I want to scream.

I've only made it about two feet from the station's exit, and I don't even know where Finn is. He's probably already found the Winston Churchill statue and hasn't even noticed I'm gone. When he does, he's going to think I'm even more of an idiot. He'll be glad he lost me and go back on the Tube to the dorm while I sit on the side-walks of Westminster and become a hobo begging for spare change from the tourists while I figure out how to get back to Queen Victoria House.

Giant groups of people are trying to cross the street in every direction, and my head feels like it's spinning. Sitting against the wall of a building, I lean my head against the window. I focus on studying all the different types of tennis shoes tourists are wearing. Twenty black pairs, twelve white, and two people wearing flip-flops. I bet they're all as clueless as I am. But at least they'd be going home in a week or so, whereas I'm stuck in London for what feels like forever.

"What're you doing?" a voice yells, and I snap out of staring at the sidewalk. Finn towers above me with his hands in his pockets. Relief floods over me. He actually came back to find me.

"I'm sorry," I say. "There were all these people, and I lost you, and I have no idea where I'm going." Then I add another sorry for good measure.

"Come on then, don't just sit around. I'll stay with you." Finn extends his hand and pulls me up. I take a deep breath. Everything will be okay.

"It's just this area," Finn says as I follow him through the crowd of people. He glances over at me, and I swear his lips pull into a tight smile. "There's a lot of history here, but with that, it also brings a lot of tourists. Once you get away from them, though, then you can really enjoy the city."

"Okay," I say. I can't believe Finn's actually saying more than one sentence to me. And I kind of can't believe I'm actually happy Finn's saying more than one sentence to me.

We cross the street, and I immediately recognize Big Ben and the gold building beside it. Parliament. Mike mentioned that in class. Finn and I take a picture, and I follow him down the road to our next clue: *A place of royal love where Prince William married Kate Middleton.*

Westminster Abbey! The church towers over us with

its ornate archway. I remember seeing it when I watched the royal wedding on TV. Seeing it in person feels surreal.

We lean against the iron fencing along with all the other tourists. The man next to me whips out his phone to take a selfie. I pull out my phone, too, and take a picture. Finn unfolds his list and crosses off clue number three.

I take another deep breath, not ready to fight through the crowd again to get to our next clue.

"Just give me a minute," I say.

Finn rests his arms on the fence and stares at the massive abbey with me.

"Why did you even choose to come to London City University if you're so stressed about being here?" he says, breaking the silence.

"I didn't want to come here. I won't be staying here after this year," I say, then explain how I applied to Boston Southeast University but got deferred for a year because of the scholarship. "My best friends are there having fun without me. All I want is to be with them where the only change I'd have to worry about is being an hour away from home, not a whole seven-hour plane trip away."

Finn studies the list of clues still in his hand, and I don't know if he even heard me. I'm not sure why I spilled out all my life details to him.

Finn clicks his pen and slips the list back into his pocket. As if by some unspoken agreement, we both turn to walk away from the abbey on to our next clue. Or rather, I walk next to Finn, hoping he's leading me in the right direction.

"I know what you mean," he finally says.

"You know exactly what I mean because you had to move to an entirely different continent without any say-so and go to a school you had no desire to go to?" How could he say he knows what I mean? No one else seems upset about being here. Everyone keeps acting like going to college in London is a dream come true.

"Well, not quite exactly a different continent," Finn says as we cross the street again to a spread of grass scattered with statues. "I grew up here, in London, and when I was sixteen, we moved to Liverpool. All my friends were here. I didn't know anyone. All I wanted was to move back to London."

"Yeah, but you're back here now," I say. Another person who actually wanted to be here. *Good for you, Finn.*

"And you'll get to be in Boston next year. At least it's only a year. I was in Liverpool for two years before I got to come back home. Never went back for a visit or anything. My dad didn't want to go back," Finn says and kicks at the dirt as a family of tourists walks by. "You know, you're already kind of a Londoner if you're annoyed by the tourists."

"I just don't like it when people walk aimlessly around and get in your way no matter where I am. I mean, I'm probably like that too since I don't know where I'm going."

A light breeze tosses Finn's curls. He adjusts his glasses, even though they sit fine on his nose.

"This is the final clue for this area," he says, pointing to a statue of Winston Churchill. "Clue number four."

We snap our picture and walk back to the station in silence, dodging the groups of tourists until we're back on the train heading to the academic buildings. An older man sits across from us, reading the newspaper, and a young woman with earbuds tunes out the rest of the world around her.

"It's a hard change," Finn says.

"Huh?" I thought there was a rule you weren't supposed to talk on the Tube. Didn't someone tell me that? Or did I just assume since it's always so quiet?

"The move," Finn says. "Moving to any new place against your will."

"It's fine," I lie. "Really, it is." I'm sure he's only trying to make me feel better after I dumped all my emotions on him.

I watch Finn shift beside me in the train window's reflection. He turns on his phone and immediately shoves it back into his pocket.

"It's not fine because I saw how miserable you were in Westminster. That's exactly how I felt in Liverpool. Everything seems fine, then everything changes." Finn takes a deep breath. "It's not fine."

The train jerks to a stop at a station, and new faces enter as the familiar ones leave. The old man flips a page in the newspaper, unfazed by the new group of people joining us.

"I miss my best friend Emily. We were going to be roommates and live in Boston together." I can't believe I'm talking to Finn about this. But I can't stop myself. "I miss my younger brother and sister, and I miss getting milkshakes at this diner downtown called Duke's, and I miss cars that drive on the right side of the road. I even miss American accents."

"When I moved to Liverpool, all I wanted was my old life, even though I knew I'd never get it back. I couldn't go play football after school with my friends. And I missed my old house and the memories we had there. Liverpool never felt like home. I was pretty miserable there."

The train comes to a stop at our station, and we ride up the escalator in silence, heading back to the academic buildings. I have my British Literature class next, which is luckily in the same building as Walking History.

"Well, I'll see you later," I say as I push open the door to the building.

Finn hovers in the doorway. "Yeah." I guess he doesn't have another class here.

In British Literature, Professor Newman, who we all call Nicola, talks more about Charles Dickens. It turns out most professors here actually prefer being called by their first names. Even though I'm trying my hardest to pay attention to Nicola's lecture, my mind can't focus. Finn and I had a normal conversation. He actually talked to me and acted like he cared. And he wasn't as rude.

He wouldn't have mentioned moving if he didn't at least have some sympathy for me. For some reason, I feel like he really did understand what I was feeling more than anyone else. Joanne was happy about the experience of living in London; Bailey became so happy here she decided to stay.

Finn was the first person I'd met so far who let me feel upset about the change.

5

Ronan shows up at our table for breakfast and slides right into the seat next to Hannah.

"Oh, hi," she says. "What're you doing here?" She twists a strand of her auburn hair around one of her fingers.

Ronan shrugs. "Thought I'd come see what's happening at this table today."

"Gag," Bailey whispers to me. "I hate listening to them flirt." I wonder if Bailey's single, like me. No one has randomly shown up at the table to sit with her, and I haven't heard her mention a significant other who's maybe back at home or at a different school.

I stir my yogurt parfait. At least the caf has a full yogurt parfait station. Actually, all their food is pretty healthy, and I have no complaints. The cooks don't slack in feeding us well, and I always look forward to what they're serving.

Bailey gathers her blonde hair into a ponytail, then leans over to whisper to me again. "They keep acting like they don't like each other when they obviously do. It's annoying." She kicks Hannah under the table and coughs. "You know there's two other people here, right?"

"Yeah, yeah," Ronan says. "Hey Bailey, what do you think about that sociology project? Hannah and I were trying to think of topics to research."

Ronan, Hannah, and Bailey launch into a conversation about sociology, throwing out terms I'd never heard of. I continue to stir my yogurt, even though I'm pretty sure all the honey and granola are mixed in.

"Good morning," Finn mumbles. He slips into the seat across from me and beside Ronan. His curls are damp, and his eyes droop. He takes off his glasses and rubs his eyes.

Bailey and I make eye contact. Even since our outing in Westminster, he's been kind to me when we've had to work together in class, but he always keeps the conversation short. Unlike Joanne and Alyssa, who I could see across the room, laughing and making plans together. Everyone else in the class seemed to be making a built-in friend with their partner, which was probably one of the intentions of the class. That was not the case for me.

"God, I hate mornings," Finn says as he fiddles with the wrapper of the singular muffin on his plate.

Mornings are my favorite part of the day. Now that I'd adjusted to the time change, I finally have my morning routine back. It helps to have one thing that still feels normal. There's something nice about waking up before anyone else and having a moment of the world to yourself. I spent this morning watching the sunrise from my window while researching where to buy art supplies in London. By the time Bailey knocked on my door, I was refreshed, awake, and ready to go.

"Finn!" Ronan slaps Finn on the back, and Finn coughs. "Glad you made it, mate."

Finn cuts his blueberry muffin in half, then into quarters. His knife continues to slice one of the quarters.

"Are you going to eat that muffin or just murder it?" I ask. My hand immediately flies to my mouth, but it's too late. I can't believe I said that out loud. It's only going to make him hate me more.

Finn puts his knife down as if he was unaware of what he was doing. His gaze doesn't meet my eyes as he shoves one of the slices in his mouth and silently chews.

"I never have much appetite in the mornings," he finally mutters to me.

That's because you just woke up, I want to say, but I catch myself this time. At least, that's what I'm assuming. He has a cup of coffee in one of the caf's paper to-go cups, but he hasn't touched it.

"Hey, Finn," Bailey says. "I'm glad you joined us." She offers him a smile.

"He would've been down here earlier if he wasn't out so late last night," Ronan says.

"Oh, piss off," Finn shoots back, but it's good-natured. Ronan laughs and reaches over to slap Finn's shoulder.

"So get this," Ronan says, his eyes popping out of his head. "I finally got Finn to go out to a club last night. Wild, right?"

"In the middle of the week?" I ask.

Hannah furrows her eyebrows. "It was a Thursday night," she says as if that explains everything.

"I've never seen anyone drink so much." Ronan laughs.

Oh. My. God. Finley Abbott was drunk in a club last night. Now that, I would've paid money to see. I can't even imagine him not being so uptight and serious. I could see him being an angry drunk. It would fit well with his personality.

Finn glares at Ronan and shoves another slice of muffin in his mouth.

"Oh, come on, mate," Ronan says. "It was good for you to get out. You had fun, at least in the beginning."

Finn snorts. "Georgia was having a full-on panic attack after my fifth shot."

"You're back together?" Bailey says.

Finn nods. "We got back together in August."

I almost choke on a piece of granola because I cannot imagine Finn with a girlfriend. I can't picture him having a conversation with her or kissing her or even saying anything affectionate. I just can't.

"That's so good to hear," Hannah says. "Tell her we said hi. I bet she's happy you're back together."

Finn offers a careless, one-shoulder shrug. "Sure."

"I can't wait to see her again," Hannah continues. "I've missed talking to her. She was always really nice to us."

"Well, yeah, that's the face she puts on," Finn mumbles. "She's good at saying what people want to hear."

Ronan furrows his eyebrows, and his eyes dart between the rest of us. "And you trust what she says to you then, mate?"

"She's honest with me," Finn says.

"That…sort of sounds like her saying what you want to hear," Ronan points out and shrugs. "But hey, that's your relationship, not mine. You'll figure it out. Look, just try to focus on having fun this year, alright? You need to take a break from being so serious all the time and fussy about your classes. The year's hardly begun, and all you want to do is study every minute you're not in a class-room. It's not like you're going to fail a class. Especially when you're the department's most promising physics student."

"I failed Walking History and have to repeat it," Finn states. "Any other questions?" His eyes dance between us all as we stare in silence. "No? Alright then. If you'll excuse me, I'm going to go to the toilets."

Finn gathers his trash and leaves before any of us have time to say anything else.

"What's his deal?" I say as soon as Finn's out of earshot.

Ronan scratches at his eyebrow. "I thought last night would be good for him. But his girlfriend's being all weird around him. She was losing her mind when she realized Finn was drunk. As in, she was full-on screaming at him at one point. Finn and I were actually having a good time, then he just kind of shut down and let her go at him. It was super uncomfortable."

"That's so strange," Bailey says. "They always seemed so happy together."

Bailey explains that Georgia goes to a different university in London but that she was always in the dorms visiting Finn or eating dinner with him last year. She'd been around a lot, and he always seemed to be in a good mood around her.

"But at the end of the year, something happened between them, and they broke up. We never heard from him what went down. We didn't really see much of him those last few weeks. And now, they're apparently back together," Bailey finishes.

"Georgia was always sweet," Hannah says. "We liked her. But who knows? After they broke up, we didn't see her again. It's not like we were good friends or anything, so she had no reason to reach out to us. I guess we'll be seeing her around again."

I open my mouth to ask a question about Georgia, but the familiar sound of plates clinking and chairs scraping against the wooden floor is my cue to head to class with the rest of the morning crowd.

Finn's already in class when I get there. His spiral notebook's open on his desk, but he hasn't written anything. I don't think he even has a pen out. Meanwhile, my hand burns from writing about the important pieces in the British Museum that Mike's been lecturing about.

"Right, I want you to think about the article I assigned for you to read," Mike says. The projector behind him is still displaying a picture of a statue from Easter Island. *Who knew that was in the museum?* "Can anyone tell me what the oldest item in the museum is?"

I stare down at my notes. Rosetta Stone, Parthenon sculptures, Roman silverware. There's silence as everyone fumbles through their notes and printed copies of their readings.

"Olduvai stone chopping tool," Finn blurts out. He doesn't meet Mike's eyes, and I'm shocked he's even participating in class.

"Very good, Mr. Abbott," Mike says. He gives Finn a nod of approval. "That's exactly what we'll be looking for today."

That wasn't even in our readings. I swear I read every word in the article Mike sent us, and I never once read anything about a chopping tool. I'm positive that name would've stood out to me.

Luckily, the British Museum is only a few blocks over from our academic building, so we walk down as a class. Mike acts like our personal tour guide, pointing out sites along the way and telling us more facts about the museum.

When we arrive, I'm amazed. Even though Mike showed us plenty of pictures in today's lecture, the ancient Greek-style pantheon still manages to take my breath away. The marble columns tower over us, making me feel small as we follow Mike inside. Once inside, the vast building swallows us whole. The glass-patterned ceiling, along with the twin white staircases, make me feel like I've been transported to another world.

Mike leads us to the Early Humans section. The glass cases are lined with rocks that are labeled as ancient tools. How did people even know these were old tools and not some random rocks? Mike points out the Olduvai stone chopping tool and it's a letdown. It looks just like all the other rocks in the case. Mike mentions a few other tools on display then leads us back to the main lobby.

"Right, so that's it for today," Mike says to our class as we gather around him in a circle. "I'd highly encourage you to spend the remainder of our class time here and look at other artifacts. There are a lot of cool things here. Otherwise, you're free to go."

The class disperses to the different wings of the museum. Joanne and Alyssa walk up the grand staircase to check out the gift shop. Finn lingers at the edge of the group, biting his nail as if considering what to do. I wish I could explore the museum with Joanne and Alyssa, but I don't want to waste time in the gift shop. I'm not in the mood to get lost in the museum, so I head to the wing straight ahead of me. Ancient Egypt. At least that sounds interesting.

I walk around the wing, not paying much attention until I've made it into a section with preserved mummies. It's weird that these glass cases actually have a dead human's body on display for anyone to see. Probably not what the Egyptians thought would happen to them. Then again, if they're dead, they don't know any difference.

"Of all the things, you pick dead bodies to look at? How morbid, Olivia."

His voice catches me off guard. Finn stands beside me with his hands in his pockets.

"Did you follow me?" I ask.

"I wanted to apologize," he says. "Maybe I've given off a poor impression. I know this year's probably over-whelming for you, and I probably haven't helped with that situation."

"No, you haven't," I blurt out. Finn's face flushes red. *Why can't I ever think before I speak?* "But, I mean, I guess you have your reasons. Failing this class."

He shakes his head. "I don't want to talk about that. It's a done deal."

"Okay then." I move on to the next mummy, feeling Finn's lingering presence behind me.

"I truly do understand what you're feeling," he says. "Even if it's not quite the same circumstances. I really am sorry for being rude."

"So you thought I was some dumb American," I say.

He tries to hide a smile, which confirms my suspicions. "Ha! You totally did."

"I was just bitter about being in this class again. I love Mike, but I don't really fancy repeating his class." He runs his fingers through his perfect curls.

"How did you even fail this class? It's not like it's hard," I say. *Ugh, why can't I keep my mouth closed?*

"I didn't go and find any of the sites," he says. "My partner was left all on his own. Alfie Robinson, if you ever see him around. He hates my guts."

"But why didn't you go?" We dodge a group of tourists gathered around a mummy mask.

Finn lets out a long sigh. "Honestly? I couldn't bear to go out in the city. All I wanted was to be back in London, and suddenly, once I was back, it didn't feel like home anymore. I never went out anywhere besides school buildings. My dad almost made me take the spring semester off and go back to Liverpool. But there was absolutely no way I was going to do that."

"What if Bartonsville doesn't feel the same anymore once I'm home?" I mutter to the mummy that's on display in front of me.

"It's not going to be the same," Finn answers. "Once you leave a place, it keeps going without you. Like these mummies. If they were to come back to life and go back to Egypt, they'd be shocked." He cracks a smile as if he's said the funniest thing.

"That's different."

"Way to ruin a joke," he says with a shake of his head.

We carry on in the museum. Finn takes me to all the points of interest, rambling on about historical facts. It's like he's a walking textbook, spitting out whole stories and pieces of information at each exhibit. It makes sense now that he'd known the Olduvai stone chopping tool was the oldest thing in the museum. He could work here.

"These are all artifacts from the time of the Vikings," he says, pointing to one of the glass cases. "It's amazing that some of these artifacts are just like what we use today. Like this Viking comb."

"How do you even know all this stuff?"

"I came here on school field trips quite often," he says. "And the museum's free, so I used to come here a lot after school to see everything I learned about in history class and see what else I could learn while I was at it. I used to come almost once a week. Until I moved."

"Why did you move?" I ask.

Finn keeps walking and doesn't make eye contact. "My dad. He changed jobs."

I nod. Something out of his control that he couldn't change no matter how much he might have wanted to. As we make our way back to the main lobby, I can't help but think about how much Finn just might understand how I've been feeling.

"Oh my god," I say after glancing at my phone. "I missed my British Literature class."

I've never deliberately skipped school, and I swore to myself I'd never miss a college class unless I was too sick to get out of bed. It's the beginning of the year, and now Nicola is going to think I don't care about school.

Finn must see the wave of panic that rushes across my face. "It'll be okay," he says.

"Says the one who failed a class," I say. "Doesn't attendance count as part of your grade?"

Finn stands in front of me, blocking me from walking any farther out of the museum.

"Olivia. Take a deep breath. It's completely my fault. I didn't realize how long we were here."

I try to breathe, but thoughts flood my mind. What if I missed something important? What if there was a pop quiz? Oh god, what if I'm behind in class now?

"I'll email Nicola," Finn says. "I took her class last year. I'll take the blame and say we were busy working on our project."

Relief floods my body as I tell Finn thank you about a million times. I can't believe he's covering for me.

"If you don't have another class, perhaps we should knock out some more items on the list," Finn says. He pulls out his folded list from his backpack. "Number fourteen is Covent Garden, which isn't too terribly far from here. Shall we?"

I'm not sure I want to spend more time with Finn than I have to, but I feel like I owe it to him to try to get work done. Especially since he was going to take care of my absence.

"Okay," I find myself saying. "Let's go to Covent Garden."

SURE ENOUGH, THE NEXT TIME I HAVE BRITISH Literature, Nicola pulls me aside after class.

"I hear you have Finn Abbott as your partner," she says. She sits on the table and swings her feet. She's a young woman who always wears bright colors. Today, she has a canary-colored skirt on and earrings shaped like sunflowers.

I nod. I'm waiting for her to get to her point and tell me I shouldn't be skipping classes, and I'm acting like a horrible student.

"He told me you both got distracted while working on a history project." She gives me a sympathetic smile. "He's a good person to have as a partner. Finn's one of the best students I've ever had."

So Finn failed Walking History but can tell me every detail of every artifact in the British Museum. And now he's Nicola's star student. And, according to Hannah, he's super smart. It was starting to look like he was good at everything academic except being someone's Walking History partner.

Nicola continues, "His writing is some of the most powerful I've ever read. He's got a deeper understanding of the world than most people I know." She smiles. "I'm glad he's your partner."

On the first day of classes, Nicola had us write a few paragraphs about ourselves and why we chose London City University. Something about her personality made me feel comfortable about sharing exactly how I was feeling. She'd never mentioned our writing, but something made me feel like she was referencing it now. Maybe even what Finn had written when he took her class last year.

"He's been...good," I say, because overall, he had been. He hadn't ditched me or refused to go to any of the sites like he said he did last year. And at least he tried to be a little sympathetic toward me. I doubt someone like Joanne or Alyssa would relate to moving somewhere you didn't want to go. They both seemed over the moon about being in London. And Finn did spend hours touring around a museum with me.

"You're lucky, Olivia," Nicola says. "Let me know if you need anything at all, ever. And don't worry about this absence. But next time, please keep an eye on the clock."

"I will," I say. "Thank you."

When I arrive back at Queen Victoria House, I'm greeted by Gabriel's loud clicks on the front desk keyboard.

"Hi, Gabriel," I say.

"Olivia! Here to save me from the boredom of desk duty," Gabriel says. It's become my routine to chat with Gabriel on the days I have British Literature since he's always on duty, and I finish classes early.

I set my backpack down and sit in one of the red plush chairs in the lobby. It's actually a nice space. Sunlight always floods the space from the large back window. I'm curious why no one ever uses it.

"So," I say. "I found this modern art museum called the Tate. Is that close by?"

Gabriel laughs. "It's not within walking distance, but nothing a Tube journey can't do for you."

"Want to go with me?" I ask.

Gabriel shakes his head. "Absolutely not. Sorry, my Residential Life duties end there. You couldn't pay me to go to an art museum. I'm glad to do just about anything else with you, though."

I could take the Tube myself to class now, but that was about it. I'd yet to learn the different lines and where to change stations. I hadn't really needed to learn since I'd left all the public transport navigating up to Finn. I guess that was the disadvantage of having a Londoner for a partner.

"You'll get there," Gabriel says. "Just give it some time."

"I don't know. By the time I'm comfortable going out on my own, it'll be time for me to go home."

Gabriel throws his hands up. "You've got to enjoy your time here. You'll get to go home eventually."

I groan. "But I want to go home now."

"Winter break will be here before you know it," he says. "Go do something fun in the meantime."

"You're sure you don't want to go with me?" I say, wiggling my eyebrows.

"I'm positive. Besides, I've got band practice almost every day this week."

That was another thing I'd learned about Gabriel from our afternoon chats. He's in a band with some guys at a nearby university. He played one of their songs one day for me. I expected something alternative sounding, but Gabriel's music was different. It was a little more on the rock side than I usually prefer, but it was pretty good. It was like the kind of song you'd hear playing on repeat on the radio's summer top hits.

"Have fun making music," I say and grab my backpack. I've got some reading to do for British Literature. And if I can get that done, I'll have some time to call my dad before heading to dinner.

"See you later," Gabriel says, and I wave as I walk down the hall.

———

After hours of forcing myself to power through my homework and ignoring my growling stomach, it's finally time for dinner. I lock my door right as another door creaks open. Finn walks out with his tan backpack slung over his left shoulder.

"Hi, Olivia," he says as he locks his door.

"Heading to dinner?"

"I was, erm, actually going to the library." He points to his backpack. "Physics homework. But maybe I should stop for some dinner."

"Um, yes, you probably should. Were you really going to skip dinner?"

"Physics is hard," he says. "And very time-consuming. But I'll come with you and stay for a little bit."

We walk out of Queen Victoria House and into the North London air. The evenings have gotten chillier, and I'm glad I grabbed a sweatshirt before I stepped out. It's my favorite teal, baby-blue, and white, chunky, striped sweatshirt I'd found in a thrift shop with Emily and Ryan. Actually, Ryan was the one who found it on the rack and said it screamed my name.

"Thanks for whatever you said to Nicola," I say as we walk down the private driveway. "She's not even going to count this absence against me."

The setting sun's rays highlight Finn's curls. Golden hour, as Emily used to describe it.

"I knew she wouldn't mind," Finn says.

"She couldn't stop saying all these good things about you."

Finn adjusts his backpack on his shoulder. "It's just because I took her for British Literature and Creative Writing. She got to know me pretty well."

"So you actually went to those classes and did the work?"

"Oh, piss off," he says in the same tone he used before with Ronan.

I can't help myself from smiling. A few weeks ago, he would've told me to piss off for real. And now, he's saying it in a sarcastic, friendly way.

We reach the caf, and Finn pulls the door open. Inside, the warmth surrounds us, and a scent that reminds me of Thanksgiving fills the air. No matter what they've cooked, it's guaranteed to be delicious. Finn follows me to our usual table and sets his backpack down beside me instead of the open seat next to Ronan.

"Get the curry if they have it tonight," he says. "It's absolutely delightful."

Even though I can't stand spicy things, I follow Finn to the Indian station and get a full helping of curry. As we walk back, Finn explains to me how London has such a diversity of cultures and an especially large Indian population.

"You can't get better curry unless you go to India itself," he says as we sit down.

Bailey, Hannah, and Ronan are in the middle of some conversation about some girl named Shelby, another second-year, and her gross boyfriend, Frederick. People who I, of course, don't know.

"Finn," Ronan says, fist-bumping him across the table. "Why'd you bring your backpack, mate?"

Finn sets down his plate and pulls a notebook out of his backpack. "Physics is bloody killing me."

A snort of laughter escapes from my nostrils. Bloody.

Finn nudges me with his fist. "What's funny?"

"Oh, nothing." My eyes catch on the pen he's twirling between his fingers, waiting for me to finish before he gets to work. "It's just…the way that you're holding your *bloody* pen."

He shakes his head and writes some physics equations. "My god, Olivia." The corner of his lip tugs upward ever so slightly. And just as quickly as it appeared, it's gone, and his face settles back into its typical neutral set.

Bailey's eyes meet mine, and she raises her eyebrows. She motions her head in Finn's direction, and I shrug.

"You seem like you've adjusted better," Bailey says. "You don't have a look of absolute panic and dread on your face when I see you."

Was it really that obvious? I thought I was hiding my strong desire to go home as best as I could. But now that I've gotten into a routine, it feels like I've been in London for months. It's been weeks since I've talked to Emily and Ryan. But they also hadn't reached out to me. A wave of panic rushes through me. But home wouldn't change. Home would always be home. Things wouldn't be different like Finn had said. Hopefully not.

"Things are getting better here," I say. I take a bite of my curry, the warmth from the dish filling my body.

"See, I told you," Bailey says. "Remember, you always

have a choice in your outcome. You can always choose to stay here and not go back to Boston."

"I'm not *that* adjusted. Boston's still home." Because, in the end, it is. Emily and Ryan would still be there, and I'd be at the same college. Everything would be fine.

"I'm just saying," Bailey says. "You never know."

Beside me, Finn's notebook receives his undivided attention, and his hand moves across the page at the speed of light. His bowl of curry sits off to the side, still half full. He sighs and puts his head in his hand.

Ronan flicks a piece of his rice at Finn's head, and it gets stuck in his curls. Hannah giggles, more at Ronan than at Finn.

"Would you cut it out?" Finn says. There's an edge to his voice that wipes Ronan's smile off his face.

Ronan reaches over to pull the piece of rice out of Finn's hair. "You've got to lighten up, mate. Uni's hardly that far in, and you're already obsessing over physics."

We're all quiet, staring at Ronan and Finn as if we're watching a tennis match.

"What, is it suddenly not cool to care about doing well in your classes?" His eyes dart between us. "Is it?"

"Finn," Bailey says. "Stop."

Finn picks up his pen and writes another equation. Ronan glances at us and shakes his head.

"I don't get it," Ronan says, loud enough for all of us to hear. Including Finn, who ignores him.

Bailey taps the table like a judge ordering in the court. "Both of you. Please. Can we not do this again this year?"

Small talk fills the rest of our dinner in an attempt to make conversation. Finn ignores us all for physics. I thought him coming to dinner would mean he'd at least talk for a little bit before he went to the library. But there's not another word out of him. Hannah and Ronan keep their conversation light, and Bailey tells me more about her hometown in California until Finn packs up and leaves, only muttering a quiet goodbye.

———

"What was up with that?" I ask Bailey as we're walking back to the dorm. Hannah and Ronan had decided to go get ice cream.

Bailey sighs. "They're good friends, but they have such different personalities. Finn's always been kind of serious and closed off. He's a super nice guy, but he gets in these really intense moods when suddenly his schoolwork is the most important thing. Ronan told Hannah that during finals last semester, he had to make sure Finn was eating and sleeping. Otherwise, he'd study to the point of exhaustion."

"Ronan has a point about him needing to lighten up then," I say.

"Yeah, Ronan's always getting on him about having fun and going out and doing stuff," Bailey continues. "It's all good-natured, but sometimes Finn takes it all the wrong way."

Bailey scans her keycard at Queen Victoria House's

door. Gabriel's typing away on his laptop at his desk while eating takeout and we both say our hellos.

"Another food delivery kind of night," Gabriel says. "Best Thai food in North London. Highly recommend it."

"I'll have to try it," I say.

Once we're down our hall, I say, "I like him."

"Gabriel?" Bailey asks.

"Yeah. He's always nice to me."

She smiles. "He's a little weird. We have French together and he's always fooling around with his vocabulary pronunciation. But it's all good fun." We're in front of her door at the end of the hall. "I'll see you later."

I settle back into my way-too-bland dorm room and massage my face with my face mask gel. Things were getting better here, I had to admit. But London still wasn't home. It never would be, but I could find a way to make it work in the meantime.

7

FINN STAGGERS INTO THE CLASSROOM ONE MINUTE BEFORE Walking History starts. I didn't even see him at breakfast. He's carrying a travel coffee cup, and his curls hang damp on his forehead. He sets his backpack down at his table and walks over to me.

"Hi," he says, interrupting my conversation with Joanne. "I never got to ask you if you liked the curry last night."

"It was good, yeah." *What a weird thing to ask.*

He nods as Mike walks into the room. "Good," he says, then returns to his seat.

Joanne wiggles her eyebrows. "Did you go out to dinner or something last night?"

I have to catch myself from laughing. "Hardly. Just dinner in the caf with him and some of the other second-years on my hall. And anyway, he's just my friend," I say.

Because he is. I'd never even consider dating Finn, especially since he has a girlfriend. Plus, I have Ryan at home, who I need to call this weekend. What if he's already forgotten about me? Then all my chances at true love with my best friend would be gone. But he wouldn't have helped me figure out what to take to London if he didn't care. He wouldn't have bought me a custom passport case with my initials printed on it in gold. He wouldn't have made an effort to see me right before I left. That's more than just something a good friend would do, but it's also Ryan. Maybe he would've done all that for anyone.

Mike's already on the seventh slide of his lecture, and I haven't taken a single note. He's explaining something about a place called Speakers' Corner, and I'm completely lost. At least Finn should be able to explain it to me later.

I hate myself for thinking that.

Mike discusses our site project and recaps about how far we should be. Finn and I are ahead, which is exactly what he wanted from the beginning. I glance over at him, and he's sitting in his chair with nothing on his desk, legs stretched out as usual.

Joanne groans when Mike pulls up the list. "Alyssa and I have been struggling big time," she whispers to me. "This stuff is hard."

It wouldn't be so hard if they didn't waste all their time in a museum gift shop. Or if they had a know-it-all, London-native partner.

Mike wraps up by explaining our site visit for today, Hyde Park. We've got to get there on our own and once we're there, find several items that are on the list. Finn shows up at my desk before I even finish packing up my stuff.

"Let's get to it," he says.

Hyde Park is a short Tube journey away, and I review the list until Finn nudges me that it's our stop. London's cool weather greets us as we step outside, and the sky's coated with its usual blanket of clouds, promising a sprinkle at some point in the day. Greenery sprawls in front of us, and I follow Finn down one of the many paths at the park's entrance. Soon, the view of surrounding buildings disappears, and we're engulfed in nature. Tree branches dip down to shade our path as we wind deeper into the park. I'm not even paying attention to where I am or where I'm going. Finn leads me through the park like he's been a million times. We reach a stone bridge where he points to the swans gliding in the pond below us.

"Clue seventeen," he reads. "'The bird found in Hyde Park. It's also the same bird the British Crown owns.' Legally, the monarch owns all the swans in London."

I snap a picture and we continue on through the spread of greenery. Bikers whiz past us, and a group of children giggle at a nearby playground. It's peaceful and I can't help but wonder what it'd be like if Emily and Ryan were here. Would we have picnics in the park together and ride bikes like we did in Bartonsville? Maybe we'd find a new place that's open until midnight to get milkshakes. No matter what city we were in, I'm sure our friendship would still be the same.

The path we've been taking merges into a much wider sand path as a huge brick building comes into view. Finn points to it.

"Kensington Palace," he says. "That's the final site for today."

A palace? In the middle of the park? If I were royalty, I'd want to live here where there are swans and flower gardens and spacious fields. With no sign of city life, it's like we've been plucked out of London and dropped in some fantasy world. A flower garden sprawls out beside the palace, perfect for a princess to wander about. I cross off the clue from my list and take a picture.

"Alright." I glance at the time on my phone. "We finished way ahead of schedule. I've still got an hour and a half until my next class."

A gust of wind blows, and I fight against it to fold the list and return it to my backpack. I'd have plenty of time now to figure out how to make it back to the academic building on my own. I could do it.

Finn clears his throat. "Fancy getting lunch?" he asks. "Since you've, erm, got time?"

I stop dead in my tracks, almost causing a man to bump into me. We exchange a quick sorry, then I turn to Finn. "Yes, actually," I say. "That'd be great."

As we walk across the street to a sandwich chain,

energy fills me and gives me a bounce in my step. We pick up chicken, avocado, and basil sandwiches from the case, then take them back to the park near Kensington Palace. I follow Finn's lead to a giant pond where swans glide in the water, and we circle until we find an open bench. Dogs run with their tongues hanging out, and some small children sit on a nearby bench with their mother, laughing at the pigeons scattered around them.

Finn digs his nail under the sticker sealing his sandwich's box. "You don't get this kind of quality food in America," he says jokingly.

I do have to admit, the sandwich is pretty good for a chain restaurant. But I've had plenty of other delicious sandwiches in Massachusetts. It's not *that* impressive.

"How would you know?" I question. "We have good food."

"Yeah, like triple-decker burgers. I spent the summer in Los Angeles. I know nothing compares." He rolls his eyes and takes a bite. "Mmm. And you want to go back to the States at the end of the year."

"Says the one who came back home after moving away," I joke.

"Yeah," he says, quieter. He shoves another bite of sandwich into his mouth and fiddles with a rip in his sandwich box. "Have you been to a pub yet?"

I shake my head. "I haven't exactly made much of an effort to go anywhere on my own."

His eyes go wide. "Are you serious? Do they not take

the American group during orientation? There's a great one down the road from Queen Victoria House if you'd fancy going tonight?" He shakes his head. "I can't believe you haven't tried a pint yet."

"I'm down. I'll invite Hannah and Bailey and Ronan."

"Oh. Erm, yeah." Finn scratches at his eyebrow. "The more the merrier."

"We've got to get Hannah and Ronan alone together tonight," I say.

Finn furrows his eyebrows and turns to face me. "We? Who said I was involved in this setup?" His eyes burn into mine, and his hazel eyes almost seem to have gold flecks in them. Ryan's gray-blue eyes always made my heart skip a beat, but Finn's eyes could give Ryan a run for his money.

"Aren't you and Ronan pretty good friends? Give him the push to finally ask Hannah out. It's obvious they both like each other."

Finn turns to look back at the swans. "Well, aren't you the matchmaker."

"They'd be cute together. Don't you want Ronan to be happy? You're the one who's in a relationship," I say. "Don't you want that for him?"

Finn takes a bite of his sandwich. "I guess," he says, his mouth still full.

"I know!" I practically jump up, and Finn's eyes grow wide in surprise. "Bring your girlfriend tonight. That way, you'll have her to talk to, Bailey and I will talk to each other, and then Ronan and Hannah will have to couple up."

Finn shakes his head. "Georgia doesn't like it when I drink. It's better if she doesn't come," he mutters.

I shrug. "Suit yourself."

"It'd be weird anyways if everyone's coupled up except you and Bailey," Finn says.

"No, it wouldn't," I say. "Besides, I have someone back at home. Ryan."

Finn nods. "Right. Your boyfriend?"

I immediately regret saying that. Ryan wasn't mine, and there was no guarantee he ever would be. He'd sent a few texts since I'd arrived in London to check in, but not much has come of that. Though Ryan and I had never been big texters; our best conversations had always happened when we'd been together. We would jokingly play Would You Rather and make up stupid questions like, *Would you rather sneeze to laugh or burp to laugh?* Eventually, Ryan would ask something like, *Would you rather know what your future looks like ten years from now but not be able to have it, or be able to alter something from your past but not know how it'd impact your future?*

Once Ryan asked something like that, our game would turn into a deeper discussion about which choice we thought was obviously the right one. Then we'd end up on a whole tangent about life. It was in conversations like that where I learned that Ryan was afraid of getting Alzheimer's like his grandmother, believed in karma, and thought artificial intelligence was going to be society's downfall. At the end of these conversations, I always went home feeling even closer to Ryan than before. Ryan and Emily were probably having those conversations during late nights in their dorms.

Before long, I'd be back together with them. After being apart for so long, Ryan and I were bound to have plenty to talk about. Who knew what could happen then?

"Okay, so I don't have a boyfriend back home," I tell Finn. "But I have someone who I'm not giving up hope on."

"Right, so you're still single. Again, making it weird if everyone who's there is on a date except you and Bailey," Finn says.

"So Bailey's not dating anyone, right?" I mentally list the few people I know at this school. "What about Gabriel?"

Finn chokes on his sandwich. "Gabriel?" His eyes seem to fill up the lenses of his glasses. "You want to set Bailey up with *Gabriel?*"

"Yeah. What's wrong with that? They'd be nice together."

"Olivia," he says, then sighs and pinches the bridge of his nose. "First of all, you barely know either one. Second, Gabriel's just weird. He used to make frog noises in the back of calculus last year."

"Hey, I talk to Gabriel every time he's at the desk. Did you know he's in a band? That automatically makes him cool."

"Really?" Finn says. "If I knew that's all it took, I would've taken up the electric guitar."

I lightly shove his shoulder. "I think once they get to know each other, they could work. Bailey's into indie music. I'm inviting him tonight."

"Sure, whatever you say. But I'm taking absolutely no blame when this doesn't work out."

I point my finger at him. "*If* it doesn't work out. Because it totally will."

We gather up our sandwich boxes and toss them in a nearby garbage can. Finn shoves his hands in his pockets. "Well, I guess we'll see what happens tonight then."

"Trust me on this," I say. I dig out my phone and open up the Maps app to try to figure out how I'm going to get back to the main academic building for British Literature.

Finn glances at my phone. "I've actually got to go and meet with my physics professor," he says. "Question on last night's homework. I'll head back with you, then meet you in the hall tonight before we go out. With everyone else."

———

Finn knocks on my door later that evening. He's changed into a dark gray, cable-knit sweater. I hope he remembers we're going out to have fun tonight and not spending the evening studying.

"Your room's so bare," Finn says as he walks in. He

scowls at the empty walls. "Why haven't you decorated it?"

"Because it's only temporary," I say. I return to my mirror to finish putting on my makeup.

"You do know they have stores here where you can buy things," Finn says. "There are inexpensive ones too."

My reflection stares back at me as I put on mascara. "Yeah, I know. I just haven't gotten around to buying things yet."

"God, and you still have the duvet they give you." He flops onto my bed. "Leave it to you, Livy."

I whip my head around so fast my mascara wand streaks across my face. *Livy.* No one's ever called me that before.

"Erm, you've got black stuff on your cheek," Finn says, gesturing to his face to show me where. He kicks his shoes off, revealing his navy socks dotted with little green fish, and stretches his legs out on my bed. Not what I would've expected, but it's adorable he picked patterned socks.

I turn back to the mirror and smudge the mascara even more until I can get it off. As I touch up my foundation, I watch Finn through the mirror, and our eyes meet. I break our gaze and focus on putting the lid back on my foundation. One more quick glance, and he's still watching. His hazel eyes, framed by his tortoiseshell glasses, are staring into mine.

"I'm hurrying, I promise," I say. I add a bit of pale

pink lipstick and let my hair down from my ponytail. "Okay. Ready."

"You look great," Finn says. He slips his shoes back on. "Let's go."

The pub is dark and musty inside but comfortable. The lights don't contribute much, and locals gather at tables, sharing pints and conversation. It's like I'm sitting in my grandfather's living room that's filled with leather chairs and antique, wooden tables.

"For you," Finn says, setting a pint of cider down in front of me. "Cheers to Olivia for finally trying cider for the first time!"

We all clink glasses, and Hannah and Ronan launch into a conversation about some TV show they've discovered they both like. They've been talking a lot more, and Bailey said she saw them walking back from sociology together. I glance at Finn as if to say, *Look at them*.

"What do you think?" Finn says, pointing to my cider and ignoring my glance.

"It's not bad," I say. I take another sip. "It's like carbonated apple juice."

Finn laughs and shakes his head. "Drink up."

"I'm so glad I didn't have desk duty tonight," Gabriel says. He takes a gulp of his cider. "Thanks for including me, Olivia."

Finn rolls his eyes, and I kick him under the table.

"We're all so glad you could come," I say. "Hey Bailey, what's the band you were telling me you like?"

Bailey's eyes light up. "Mechanical Love. They're doing a show in London next week, and I'm going to try to get tickets."

"Mechanical Love?" Gabriel leans toward Bailey. "No way. They're such an inspiration to me."

"Oh my god, did you all know Gabriel's in a band?" I ask. Blank stares all around. "Gabriel, you should tell Bailey about it. Bailey loves music."

Gabriel forces a smile. "Yeah, we play a few gigs here and there. We're kind of like Mechanical Love. Really, they're a huge inspiration for me since they're from Birmingham, which is my hometown. So it's cool to see them become so successful in the indie music scene."

"Oh, that's cool," Bailey says. She digs her phone out of her little white crossbody bag and sends a quick text before shoving it back inside.

I raise my eyebrows at Finn, but he shakes his head.

"How's Walking History going?" asks Bailey.

"It's fine," Finn says. He takes a long sip of cider. He puts his elbows on the table and cradles his head in his hand. "It would've been better if I'd bloody passed it last year, but at least I've got Olivia this time."

Warmth rushes through my body, and I can't stop the smile that spreads across my face. I couldn't wait to tell Emily and Ryan about the friends I was making here…if I could ever get in touch with them. I called Emily two nights ago and got a text back saying she was sorry she missed my call. That's it. No, *I'll call you tomorrow* or *Let's talk soon.*

"I'm glad I have you guys," I say. "You've made this transition so much easier."

I glance at my phone to check to see if either of them has written anything. Nothing. Their faces smile back at me on my lock screen background. I remember that day like it was yesterday. It was two days after our high school graduation, and we'd gone down to this neighborhood ice cream shop that we'd grown up eating at. We spent three hours there talking about how weird things were going to be and how much our lives were going to change in the next few months. But in that moment, we still felt like we had an infinite amount of time, like college was still so far off in the future.

Emily insisted on getting a picture of the three of us sitting on a bench outside the shop. Our hair was messy from riding in Ryan's convertible, but it didn't matter. Even Emily didn't care that her hair was a frizzy mess. We were laughing and one hundred percent natural in that picture. My head was turned, facing Ryan, and I was laughing while his eyes were fixed on his vanilla ice cream cone. Emily stood behind us with her arms wrapped around us. Afterward, each of us immediately set that picture as our lock screens. I wonder if they still have it as theirs now.

"Who are they?" Finn asks.

"Nosy much?" I tease. "They're my best friends from

home." My best friends from home, who I've had zero communication with for the last few weeks.

"The guy?" Finn says, pointing at Ryan. "Does he happen to be the one you're secretly pining for?"

"Well, when you put it that way…"

Finn puts his hands up. "I'm just repeating what you told me earlier. Who's the girl?"

"Emily."

Up until now, we'd never gone a day without talking, ever. Even if we didn't see each other that day, we still had stuff to talk about and catch each other up on. We used to know every detail about each other's lives. Now we knew nothing. Once our classes got into full swing and we were in different time zones, it was harder to schedule phone calls. Our daily calls the first few days in London had turned into weekly Tuesday afternoon chats. But when Emily started getting involved with a club soccer team, Tuesday afternoon chats turned into a *Can I call you later?* And now, it'd been weeks since we'd talked.

"I bet you miss them," Bailey says. "My first year was so hard with the big time difference. My friends from home still keep in touch, but it's different. You'll get to the point where the people here are the friends you end up talking to more and missing when you're apart."

Finn's words repeat in my mind. Once you leave, things are never really the same. But he was back in London, like he wanted to be all along. But what about all the friends he left behind? Did they forget about him when he moved back?

Hannah and Ronan share a glance, and Hannah nudges an inch closer to Ronan.

"Thanks, Olivia, for inviting all of us," Bailey said. We lock eyes and I'm certain she's thinking the same as me. This might be the final push these two needed to get together.

One couple on their way to being together, one more to go. One that was going to take a lot more work because Gabriel hadn't said a single word to Bailey after their music conversation.

Finn sets his empty pint down. "I'm going back to the bar. Need anything? Shots, Ronan?"

Ronan jumps up. "Let's go, mate."

A minute later, Finn and Ronan are back at our table, each with another pint.

"Never take physics," he says. "Unless you want to have absolutely no social life."

"Would you shut up about physics?" Bailey says. "That's all you talk about now." I forgot Bailey and Finn have an upper-level literature class together and that I'm not the only one who gets to see him in a class.

"That's the only thing I have to talk about right now," he says. "Plus, it's really hard."

Bailey shakes her head. "Finally, something you find hard."

"So," I say. "Gabriel, don't you and Bailey have a class together?" I've got to get them talking again.

He nods. "French. We've got French together."

I glance at Finn. "Right, that's it. Weren't you saying

the other day there was an upcoming exam? Or was that Bailey? Anyway, are you two going to study together?"

Finn coughs into his fist to hide his smirk. "Bloody obvious," he says under his breath to me, and I kick him again. This time, he kicks me back.

"Ow!" I cry and whip around to him. "What was that for?"

Finn's face is only inches from mine as he leans into my ear. "Payback," he whispers, his breath sending a tingle all the way down my spine.

Before I can say anything to get the conversation back to Bailey and Gabriel, Finn's phone starts vibrating in his pocket. In a swift motion, he digs out his phone, sighs, and answers.

"Hello?" he says as if this person has been calling him twenty times in the past minute.

"No, I'm at a pub," he says tightly. The conversation at our table halts, all eyes on Finn. "Because I felt like it, simple as that…Well, it wasn't really planned. It just happened…Yes, you can come…See you soon."

Finn shoves his phone back in his pocket and sighs. "Georgia's on her way."

Hannah's face lights up like a Christmas tree. "Oh, yay!"

Any chance of my suggested study date falls off both Bailey and Gabriel's radars as Hannah and Bailey talk about how long it's been since they'd seen Georgia. Bailey and Gabriel would be more work than I thought. But I wasn't ready to give up on them yet.

"Want to do another shot with me, mate?" Ronan says.

"Alright," Finn says like it's nothing, jumping up from his seat. "Let's go. Might need more than one at this point."

I lock eyes with Bailey, and she shrugs. Hannah's laughing at Ronan as he dances his way up to the bar, dragging Finn behind him. Gabriel sits there as if he's still on desk duty with nothing to do. *Fantastic.*

A while later, Finn and Ronan stagger back to the table each holding another shot and another pint.

"Cheers," Ronan says, then they throw back their shots.

A grin breaks out on Finn's face. "I've quite lost count of how many that was," he says.

"Insane," Ronan shouts and buries his head into Hannah's shoulder. She runs her hands through his black curls. "What if we started a karaoke night here?" he says.

"No," Hannah whispers. "Let's not."

"So recently, I've been reading about the speed of light," Finn says to no one in particular.

"And?" I offer.

He can't stop himself from bursting into laughter. "It's fucking cool," he says as a small smile spreads across his face.

Gabriel raises his eyebrows. "You're studying physics, aren't you?"

Finn rests his head on his hand. "Physics is fun. But it's also bloody hard." He sighs. "Learning is *so* powerful."

"Shut up," Ronan yells. "That's all you ever want to talk about."

"I just love physics!"

"Oh god," Hannah says, nudging Ronan.

Finn lets out a soft laugh. "The speed of light. It's so cool."

Ronan claps his hands. "You're mad, mate. Absolutely mad."

Finn bursts out laughing again. I think tonight might be the first time I've ever seen him really smile. But just as quickly as his smile appeared, it disappears as he looks over to the pub's door.

A girl with long, brown curls and a face full of makeup walks in like her family owns the pub. Her heeled, black boots clink across the hardwood floor as she makes her way over to our table. She grabs a chair from an empty nearby table and forces herself in between me and Finn.

"Hi," Finn says, any excitement drained from his voice.

"Georgia," Hannah squeals. "How're you?"

Georgia flashes a smile, and of course her teeth are perfectly white. "Good to see you, everyone. It's been a while. Hannah, I absolutely *love* that top. It really looks great on you."

Finn's quiet as he sips from his pint. Georgia sets her hand (perfectly manicured with purple acrylics) on his thigh.

"What're you doing?" Georgia whispers to Finn, just loud enough for me to hear.

Finn sets his glass down. "What does it look like?"

"Finn," Georgia says. His name comes out of her mouth, crisp and edged with disappointment. "Don't you ever learn from your mistakes?"

"Can you just let me enjoy myself for once?" he says. He brings his glass to his lips and takes a long chug.

"Oh my god." Georgia rolls her eyes and twists a strand of her hair. "You really want a repeat of last week, don't you?"

I try to scoot my chair away from Georgia as much as I can, but I can only move about an inch without bumping into Bailey. I turn to try to join in on Bailey and Hannah's conversation, but Finn's voice is loud enough that we all hear him.

"Would you stop? I did learn from last week, I learned not to invite you to a pub with me again so I wouldn't have to listen to you ridicule me about every little decision I make. God!"

Finn drops his head into his hands. Again, all conversation at our table stops, though I don't think Finn or Georgia notice.

"Finn," Georgia says as she places one hand on his shoulder and uses her other to move his pint out of his reach. "You're so drunk right now. You don't really mean that. And who's going to be the one to clean up your vomit again and deal with your pissy hangover mood just like last time?"

Finn lifts his head up and glances at all of us as if we shouldn't be here right now. This is a side of the story we didn't hear about. I do feel bad for Georgia having to deal with hungover Finn. That version of him is probably one of his worst.

"It honestly wasn't all that bad," Ronan offers.

"You weren't the one cleaning it out of his clothes," Georgia shoots back. "Or trying to get him in the shower."

"You didn't have to do that," Finn murmurs. "Let's just go back to my room and call it a night." He gives us a forced smile. "I'll see you all tomorrow, have a good night."

And with that, Finn staggers up and takes hold of Georgia's hand.

"Really great to see you all," Georgia says. "We'll definitely have to catch up sometime."

"Of course," Hannah says. "That'd be great."

We watch in silence as Finn and Georgia walk out of the pub, hand in hand, without a glance back at us. We hold our breath until we see the pub door close behind them.

"What was that?" Bailey's the first to break the silence.

"That was so awkward," I say.

Ronan reaches over for the rest of Finn's pint and brings it to his lips. "She was like that last week when Finn got plastered."

"They weren't like that when I saw them last,"

Gabriel says. "When I had desk duty a few days ago, they were walking out laughing and smiling. Seemed like everything was okay."

"Is this new?" I ask.

"I'd say," Hannah says. "Even Georgia seemed off." Hannah fills me in on how much time Georgia and Finn would spend together last year and how happy their relationship had looked.

"Finn seemed pretty miserable tonight," I say.

Hannah shrugs. "They'll be fine. She's probably just jealous she didn't get invited. She'll get over it by tonight, I'm sure."

I hope whatever happened tonight was simply just one of them having a bad day. Especially if Finn just got back together with Georgia. I hope she's someone who makes him happy most days.

"Didn't help that Finn's drunk," Ronan adds. "He always says the wrong things, and seeing him like that annoys Georgia. They'll work it out. They always do."

"I'm not so sure," Bailey says.

We launch into a conversation about Finn's relationship and debate if it's an unhealthy relationship or if Georgia is just having an off day.

"At least she didn't scream at him this time," Ronan says. "That was really awkward when I went out with them."

After that, our conversation quickly jumps to our bad first dates. Gabriel tells a story about how he thought he was being stood up on his first date with a girl, only to realize he'd had the day wrong and the date was the following day. Hannah talks about a date she went on where the guy's voice was so nasally she couldn't handle it. Even though we laugh sharing our stories, my mind can't help but wander back to Finn's relationship. I wonder what they're doing right now, if he's happy with Georgia, or if they're arguing. Then I wonder why I even care. Like Ronan said, they'll probably work out whatever's going on. It's not my place to say anything to Finn.

8

It's a cloudy Saturday. At the beginning of the semester, we were lucky when London provided us with endless sunny days. But now, as the leaves begin to change, cloudy skies have replaced the sun. I don't mind, though. It's the perfect weather for curling up with a good book or the massive pile of homework we have as midterm season approaches.

I flip through my notes for my communications class and try to get my brain to absorb the hundreds of definitions that'd be on my exam. I've been at it for hours now and feel like I've only made a little progress.

A single knock at my door startles me, especially since this morning Bailey, Ronan, and Hannah all made plans to go to Camden and visit the market. Unfortunately, with all my homework and studying, I'd had to skip out.

I jump up from my desk and open my door. Finn stands there holding a single notebook, his curls still damp from a shower. His baggy, gray sweatpants seem strange compared to his normal class attire. And, oh my god, he has navy slippers on.

"Hi," he says. He adjusts his glasses. "I, erm, didn't know if you were around. Was wondering if we could study for the Walking History midterm?"

I raise an eyebrow. "Aren't you already the expert on Walking History?"

"Erm," Finn says. He fiddles with his backpack strap. "I figured you might need some help?"

I let out a laugh. "Wow, Finn, how kind of you." But I step aside, smiling as I let him in. My white room suddenly feels smaller with someone else in here. He places his slippers at the door, then makes himself at home by tossing himself on my bed and wrapping my lilac blanket around him.

I settle back in at my desk. Finn is now full-on lying on my pillows, getting my pillowcase all wet from his damp curls.

"You okay?" I ask.

"I'm just dandy," he says.

He pulls the blanket closer to his shoulders, which uncovers his feet, and he groans.

"So, did you want to study—"

"No," Finn says. He fluffs up my pillow and closes his eyes.

"Okay."

On that note, I'll no longer be bothering Finn. I return to my definitions, reading them over again and again. I'm going to ignore that Finn's randomly taking a nap on my bed. Totally normal. Not weird at all.

"I'm really hungover right now," Finn moans out of the blue. He lets out another groan. "I'm sorry."

He sits up and wraps the blanket around himself like a cape. So this is the pissy, hungover Finn Georgia was talking about. It's not like he's *that* horrible.

"So you don't actually want to study at all then?"

"I need to. For physics. And calculus. I should've last night, but…" Finn rubs his head. "Now my brain's knackered."

"About last night," I tentatively start. "Is everything alright with your girlfriend?"

Finn deflates. "Shit, Livy." He sighs and throws his head back, which results in him smacking his head against my wall. He curses under his breath. "We're fine."

I turn back to my list of definitions and flip to the next page in my notebook.

"You know, if you ever want to talk about it, I'm always here for you," I say. "I'm not friends with Georgia like the others are, so nothing would ever get back to her."

He doesn't say anything, and I'm not going to push it. It's not my place. I reach for the stack of index cards on my desk and start writing down the next set of definitions I need to memorize.

"God, my head's killing me," Finn moans. "I'm going to stop by the main desk and see if they've got anything. It's practically like a chemist shop down there."

"Have fun with that," I say.

"Piss off," he says as he walks out the door.

I focus my attention back on my homework. I don't even understand why we have to take gen-ed classes that have nothing to do with our major. It's so boring.

My phone vibrates on my desk. When I go to answer, I almost drop it when I see it's Ryan video calling. I take a deep breath and unlock my phone. I'm greeted with Ryan's huge smile. He's holding the phone so close to his face that it fills my entire screen.

"Olivia," Ryan yells. He pulls the phone back from his face, and it's just him. No Emily or Maddie or whoever Ryan's roommate is in the background. I've got to keep my composure. But I smile as wide as possible before I can stop myself.

"I'm so glad you called," I say with *way* too much enthusiasm.

"I miss you," he says, making my body sing. "How're things?"

Ryan and I catch up with our classes, and he tells me about his disaster of a roommate. We're laughing about how loud his roommate snores when Finn walks straight into my room without knocking.

Which I normally wouldn't mind because why would he knock when I knew he was coming right back?

Except now I wish he would have.

"So," Finn says.

I wave my hand at him to shoo him away and whip around. Ryan's still talking about roommate horror stories, and I pray he didn't see or hear Finn. Finn scowls, plops down on my bed, and lets out a long, drawn-out sigh. I move out of my camera frame and mouth, *Shut up* at him. Finn rolls his eyes and curls back up under my blanket.

"So that's why I feel like I barely get any sleep," Ryan finishes.

"At least that's the one advantage I have over you. No roommates on my hall," I say. "Hey, uh, I've actually got to go. I'm supposed to be meeting a partner for a project. So good to talk to you, Ryan. Call again, okay?"

We say our goodbyes and hang up.

"Really?" Finn says.

I toss a crumpled-up piece of notebook paper at him. "I wasn't about to tell him you were here."

"Whatever," Finn says, tossing the balled-up paper up and down. "You need to do something with your room. It's depressing me."

"By the time I decorate it, I'd just have to pack it back up and take it home," I say.

"To Boston, with Ryan and Emily." His eyes focus on the paper ball. Up and down, up and down.

"Yeah. I'll decorate my room once I'm there with them next year."

"You're still holding out for them," he says.

"Huh?" I put down my pencil and spin around in my desk chair.

"Ryan. He's nothing more than a friend, but you're

still holding out for more. And Emily, you're still hoping she'll be the exact same person she was when you left."

I'm sorry, Finn, but who gave you the right to tap into my thoughts?

"What?"

Finn pushes himself into a seated position. "Your phone background. The way your face looked when you were talking to Ryan. The fact that you're still not quite satisfied with being here. It's obvious, Livy. To me, at least."

My mouth gapes open, but no words come out.

"I can see it because I've been that same way. I had friends here who I never saw again when I moved back. It's weird. I'm still not as happy in London as I thought I'd be."

"But Ryan and Emily, I've known them for forever. They're not going to change that much."

He goes back to tossing his makeshift ball. "Maybe not much, but people do change. It's just something we all struggle to accept. But it's life." He flips open his note-book to a page filled with writing. "Georgia was one of my good friends from childhood. She actually lived right down the street. But even she's changed during the time I was in Liverpool. We broke up over the summer, and now that we're back together, it's different."

"Is that why you didn't seem too happy around her last night?" I say gently.

"I was drunk," Finn murmurs. "Nothing you say when you're drunk is true."

"Why is it that I've always heard the opposite of that phrase?" I whisper.

Finn takes his glasses off and rubs his eyes. "The thing is, with Georgia, she was one of the only people I knew when I came back to London. By the time I came back here for uni, my old friends from school had all gone elsewhere. So it was nice to have someone familiar again. And she knows me better than anyone else. She really understands me. But she's also changed. She's just more dramatic now, I guess."

Finn's phone dings, and he digs it out of his pocket. "Speaking of," he mutters. He stares at his phone as if he's trying to decode hieroglyphics. "I've got to go," he says, then sighs.

"So, is everything okay then?"

Finn stuffs his textbooks and still-open notebook into his backpack. "It's fine," he says.

I don't want to pry for any more information that isn't mine to know, but I have my doubts everything was fixed overnight. So I give him one more chance.

"Do you really want to be around someone who's making you feel like you have to walk on eggshells?"

Finn slings his backpack over his shoulder. Yes, the answer is yes. He doesn't even have to tell me. He's already at my door, ready to leave in a matter of seconds.

"You don't understand what we have, Livy. I can't just let her go," he says. "I need her. And I know you'd do the same for Ryan. Even if it means fabricating some lie so he doesn't suspect there's another boy in your room. The reality is we're not all as perfect as we seem."

The door closes behind him, and I'm left alone in my room. I can't even concentrate on communications vocabulary anymore. Why do I even care about his relationship? Finn is my friend, nothing more. And he's right. I would do anything for Ryan. I hate him for even knowing that.

I close my notebook. My window faces out to the private drive and it doesn't take long until Finn appears. He's wearing the same T-shirt, an off-white graphic tee with a record printed on it and the words ART DECO. He's added a black sweater.

His strides are long, like he's racing to get to the Tube station. There could be a million thoughts running through his mind right now, but she's for sure his number one focus. He's almost out of sight when he stops and turns. I swear he looks back at my window for a split second. But it's probably a coincidence. His room is only two doors down from mine. He could've been checking to make sure he turned his light out or something. He turns around and is off on his way.

What could their relationship have that would make Finn drop everything to go and see her? He's so afraid of disappointing her but also so eager to see her. I pull my blinds closed. I can't be thinking about Finn and what he's doing. For right now, I've got my communications vocabulary to learn.

Finn comes into Walking History late. Like, a solid ten minutes after Mike started his lecture. The door creaks open, and everyone turns their attention to Finn. His curls are all over the place, turning all the wrong way. And he's still wearing the ART DECO T-shirt.

"Sorry," Finn mutters as he slips into his seat.

"Class starts at nine sharp, Mr. Abbott," Mike says. "Please remember to set your alarm accordingly."

Finn sinks in his seat, and his face turns the color of a tomato. "Yes, sir."

Mike continues his lecture, but I can't concentrate anymore. I can't even look at Finn. *He didn't even bother changing!* It's like he wants to rub it in my face. Yeah, people change, and your hometown will never feel the same, but at least *my* girlfriend and I are fine.

I don't know why I'm so annoyed. I mean, they've

known each other for so long. It's like what should've happened with me and Ryan. I should be happy that Finn's with the girl he loves. Although I don't understand how he can love someone he's not happy with.

Finn, as usual, has nothing out on his desk except for a paper coffee cup he's sipping from as if his life depends on it. When we make eye contact, I raise my eyebrows. *Really, Finn?* That's what I want to scream across the room at him, but he must know exactly what I'm thinking because he turns his head away and becomes fascinated by the sleeve on his coffee cup.

I hate that I'm judging him. But the red flags in his relationship are so obvious. Maybe I don't know what they have. Maybe everything really is fine. It's not my place to judge, I remind myself. As long as he's happy, that's all that matters.

Mike's voice pulls me out of my trance. I stare down at my empty notebook and realize I have no idea what his lecture was even about. "That's it for today. You're dismissed," he says. "Except Finn and Olivia, if you'll both stay back for just a moment, please."

Everyone around me gets up, and I'm left sitting there wondering what I did. I hope Mike isn't blaming me by default for Finn's lateness. My stomach feels like it's on fire as I wait for the last person to leave the room. Finn won't meet my eyes.

Mike closes the door and sits down across from us. "Finn," he says. Mike's a carefree guy, so I'm surprised his voice is suddenly so stern. "This isn't going to be a repeat of last year, is it?"

Finn's head hangs low as he stares down at his desk. "No, sir. It won't happen again."

"Olivia," Mike says, this time in his normal, cheery voice. "Has Finn been a fair partner? Has he been contributing to the assignment?"

I nod. "Finn's been great," I say a little too quickly. "We're ahead, actually."

"Right then," Mike says. "I just wanted to check in." Mike catches Finn's eye, and some sort of unspoken conversation passes between them. Finn gives Mike a tight nod as we pack up our stuff.

"That was weird," I say once we're out of the building.

Finn shrugs as if this happens every day. "Mike's always on me like that. He contacted my dad last semester when I wasn't coming to class. He means well, but I wish he wouldn't meddle."

"At least he cares?"

"Yeah, I guess. He's one of the few. So does Nicola."

We're silent as we walk down the streets of the city. I can't take it anymore. The words that have been on my mind find their way out.

"You were late because you spent the night at Georgia's," I say.

"Yes?" Finn says. "So? It's my choice and my own fault I didn't give myself enough time to get to class."

"I guess I'm just having trouble understanding," I say, feeling small. I hate confrontation. I could call out Finn all day in my head, but saying my thoughts out loud to him? Terrifying.

"Understanding what?" Finn says. He stops in the middle of the sidewalk and crosses his arms. "Why I slept with my girlfriend? What doesn't make sense there?"

I wish I'd never said anything to begin with. I don't even know what point I was trying to make. "I don't know. I guess because of everything you said yesterday. About things being different. I just want you to be happy, I guess."

"Some pros outweigh the cons. Tell me you wouldn't do the same if Ryan took the next flight into Heathrow."

"Ryan and I were never dating," I say. "And we probably never will now that I'm over here." The truth hurts to admit out loud. But really, I have no idea what Ryan's doing in Boston or who he's meeting. And how in the world would Ryan and I even be able to date when we're living in different countries? But if, for some reason, he were to show up in London tomorrow, Finn's right. I'd do anything to see him and spend time with him. I'd let go of all my rational thinking in a heartbeat.

"It's complicated, Livy," Finn says. "We have our issues, but I'm not giving up on what we have. I'm sorry."

We walk down the stairs of the Tube station, where we go our separate ways. Why was he sorry? What was he even talking about? I glance back, but he's already disappeared in the group of people heading to the Tube platform.

————

I'm sitting in my dorm that evening, drinking a chai latte, when Emily finally answers my video call. I've been trying to reach her over the past week, and the timing hasn't worked out with our schedules until tonight.

"Hi," she says. She's in her dorm, sitting on the white plush futon I helped her pick out. "It's been forever, I'm so sorry. I've been busy with soccer practice and sorority stuff. But tell me everything. Have you made any friends?"

I tell her about Hannah and Bailey but leave out Finn. After Emily flips the camera around to let me say hi to Ryan, I'm glad I did.

"Hey, Olivia," Ryan says. He's sitting on Emily's rug next to Maddie. A bowl of popcorn sits between them, along with a pile of blankets. They're having a winter movie night like we used to have in high school. I bet Emily has hot chocolate in the microwave.

Emily flips the camera back to her. "Anyway, we just wanted to say hi real quick."

"Which cheesy Christmas movie are you watching?" I can't help myself from asking. We always started watching Christmas movies whenever it got cold. That's exactly what we'd be doing if I was there.

Emily shakes her head. "We're not watching one of those. We're watching a new movie Maddie recommended. I'll let you know how it is, and maybe you can watch it with your friends."

We hang up, and I'm left in my room thinking about the three of them hanging out together. It's like they were just waiting for me to leave so they could replace me with Maddie. I'm Emily's best friend, always had been, and always would be. But now Maddie gets to come and replace me overnight? Were they happier without me around?

We don't talk the way we used to. They've moved on, but there has to be a part of them that feels like something's missing, right? That *I* was missing?

I'll be home for Christmas break in a little over a month. Once I'm back, everything will fall right back into place, and it'll be like I never left. At least, I hope so.

There's a light tap at my door. I open it to find Finn standing there with his backpack over his shoulder. He's finally changed into fresh clothes.

"Can I do homework here, if you aren't busy? The silence in my room is getting a bit loud," he says.

"Come on in." I open the door wider. I'm still a little annoyed at him for putting up with his girlfriend, but that's his issue, not mine. Plus, I could use a distraction from thinking about my friends at home.

Finn unties his shoes, revealing his navy socks, this time dotted with little yellow stars. He grabs my purple fuzzy blanket from the foot of my bed and wraps it around his shoulders. He rearranges my pillows, and once he's made himself comfortable on my bed, his physics textbook makes its appearance. Finn's hand moves across his notebook's page as if solving physics problems is as easy as completing basic addition.

I pick up my phone and reply to a text from my dad. He wrote to me to tell me how busy work is and how much quieter the house seems without me. My younger brother and sister are still at home, but it's nice to know my dad misses having me there.

"She's still annoyed," Finn says as I'm mid-sentence.

I spin around in my chair to face him. "Huh?"

"Georgia," Finn says. He sighs and drops his pen on his notebook. "She doesn't like it when I'm hungover."

I feel bad for the conversation we had after class now. "I guess it wasn't really a good night with her?"

Finn shakes his head. He's lying on his stomach now and his feet are hanging off my bed. "She makes me so mad. It's my choice if I want to get completely wasted and hungover. I don't understand why that makes her so upset. She goes clubbing practically every weekend, but if I want to go out one odd night, suddenly that's a problem. Then she complained when I said I needed to study last night. So now I'm even more behind on my work than I was yesterday. And then, that makes her upset when I'm in a bad mood. It's like no matter what, I can't win."

I fiddle with the zipper on my laptop sleeve. "I just don't think someone should be with a person who tries to make them feel bad for who they are," I whisper.

Finn rolls onto his back, his eyes making contact with me upside down. "But I've known her since I was a kid.

She knows me better than anyone else, the good and the bad. I can't imagine life without her. I don't think I'd be able to function without her."

"But…" I say. "There's always a 'but' to everything."

Finn twists his pen around. "But," he says. "She was never so controlling like this until recently. We fight, make up, then everything's okay again. That's just how things are. I knew I needed to go spend last night with her to make up for getting drunk the night before. I thought that'd make her happy."

He sighs heavily. "But I get over there and she just starts going at me and making me feel so guilty," he continues. "Especially when she saw I'd brought my textbooks. It became a whole fight about how if I hadn't gotten drunk, then I would've had more time to study. We both ended up going to bed angry. But in the morning, once my hangover was gone, we talked through things. We both apologized, and she said our relationship could only get better going forward. That's why I was late to class. So at the end of the day, I think I still love her."

"Think?" I ask. "And you fight all the time, then make up?"

He rolls back over to his stomach and props his chin in his hands. "When we were broken up this past summer, it was some of the most miserable months of my life. I really don't know if I can be without her again. Anyway, fighting's normal in any relationship. You can fight with someone constantly and still love them. Ups and downs happen all the time."

Back at home, there's this couple who own Duke's, our local diner spot I'd grown up going to. The owners, Sandy and Marc, can't take their eyes off each other. I may not know a whole lot about everlasting love, but from what I've seen with Sandy and Marc, it's exactly what I think happily ever after is supposed to look like. Every time I'm around them, it's like they've just met, even though they've been married for forty-five years. In all my years of going to Duke's, I've never once seen them fight. Sometimes Sandy would get upset because Marc forgot to order a new tub of vanilla bean ice cream, but they'd always end up making it a joke and laughing about it. Sandy even told me the key to a good relationship was someone who could make you laugh and smile in any situation. I doubt she'd agree with what Finn had just said.

"So," Finn says, breaking me from my thoughts. "Any updates with Gabriel and Bailey?"

"Nope. They say hi to each other, but that's about it. I can't get them to have a single conversation," I say.

Finn cracks a smile. "Maybe you're trying too hard to force something that isn't going to happen."

"What? No, I think they'd be good together. You've just got to give them time, Finn," I say.

"Whatever," he says, tossing a pillow at my head. "I have no reason to believe anything you say."

"What do you need then? Evidence?"

"Exactly. Come to me once you're dating Ryan," Finn says.

"Well, maybe that'll happen over Christmas break." If everything goes according to plan, Ryan could be my boyfriend once I'm back home and tell him how I feel. And maybe he'll say he feels the same way too. And we'll figure out a way to make long-distance work. After all, they always say distance makes the heart grow fonder. Whoever "they" are, I hope they're right.

10

THE FALL DAYS HAVE FADED INTO EARLY WINTER NIGHTS, and Christmas hovers right around the corner. On Oxford Street, shops are adorned with wreaths and the first of the Christmas lights are going up. I follow Hannah and Bailey down the crowded sidewalk as we shop.

"You've got to come here once they have all the lights up," Bailey says. "It's like magic."

Hannah points out a shop and we ride the escalator up to the third floor. Hannah's been saying she needs to find a new dress to wear to go out with Ronan.

"Things are getting pretty serious," Hannah says. "Thanks for organizing the pub night, Olivia. I think that helped to make some things happen."

So the pub helped set them up, but nothing had happened yet with Bailey and Gabriel. And I couldn't count Hannah and Ronan as a match I'd set up. They were already going to get together. They just needed an extra push.

Hannah holds up a little black dress and looks in the mirror. She's someone who can pull off anything. But especially this dress. The black would make her auburn waves pop and with a pair of heels…I could already see the outfit coming together.

"I'm getting this one," Hannah says. She doesn't even bother trying it on. She doesn't need to. The dress will hug her body in all the right places. It's as if it was designed for her and only just waiting for her to come buy it.

Bailey and I linger to the side while Hannah gets in line to check out.

"It's about time they got together," Bailey says. "Hannah spent all last year crushing on him. I'm surprised it took this long."

Now was my chance to do some digging. "You're not dating anyone, are you?" I ask. Because what if all this time Bailey had some long-distance boyfriend and that's why she was hardly considering Gabriel as a potential? But I'm certain she would've mentioned her faraway boyfriend in some conversation.

Bailey shakes her head. "Not at the moment, no. I was dating a friend from high school last year, but the distance was pretty hard, so it didn't work out. We broke up about a month into the first semester."

A wave of heat rushes through my body. Ryan and I

would have to be long-distance for the entire spring semester. It was only a few months, then we'd be at the same school, but still. What happened with Bailey isn't what happens to everyone. There are plenty of long-distance couples out there. I could think of at least three couples from high school who went off to different colleges and, to my knowledge, were still together. Ryan and I could manage a few months knowing that there was an end in sight.

"What about someone here?"

Bailey runs her fingers over the silver necklaces hanging up by the checkout. "I don't know. I guess no one's ever caught my attention."

Ugh, Bailey! I want to scream. "What about Gabriel?" The words escape my mouth before I can stop them.

"Gabriel?" Bailey says. "As in, Gabriel our RA?"

How many other Gabriels are there? "Yes, him."

Bailey wrinkles her nose. "He's a little weird."

"Who is?" Hannah appears beside us with her shopping bag, which is super bad timing because I haven't even gotten to explain to Bailey why Gabriel would be a good match.

"Olivia thinks I should date Gabriel," Bailey says as we walk out of the store.

Hannah's eyes go wide. "Olivia!"

"What's wrong with Gabriel?"

Hannah and Bailey make eye contact, and an unspoken message passes between them.

"Well," Hannah says. "He's a little awkward. And kind of nerdy. He's always at the front desk doing homework."

"Finn's always doing homework too," I say, suddenly feeling defensive of both Gabriel *and* Finn.

"I don't know," Bailey says. "I want someone who's fun. Someone who can let loose and enjoy the world and doesn't feel limited by where they are. I want someone who wants adventure."

"I wouldn't give up on Gabriel," I say. "Just trust me."

———

By the time we finish shopping and get back to Queen Victoria House, it's already almost dinnertime.

"I'll meet you down at the caf," Hannah says. "I'm going to go hang with Ronan for a bit."

"Let's meet in about thirty minutes?" Bailey says. "I've got to finish up an assignment that's due tonight."

Gabriel greets us when we walk in, and Bailey and Hannah smile before going to their rooms. I linger and internally scream when Bailey and Gabriel have zero interaction.

"How's it going, Gabriel?" I say and prop my elbow on the desk.

"Just finishing up a paper so I have time for band practice tonight," he says. "We're trying to secure some venues so we can do some shows in London. If we can get that gig, who knows what can happen from there." He throws his arms in the air. "Tour across the UK, then a European tour, then North America, then worldwide!"

"Remember me when you're famous," I say, and a light bulb goes off in my head. "Hey, you know Bailey loves adventure and bands. Maybe she'd be able to help with the tour."

Gabriel laughs like I've made a joke. "Maybe," he says.

"Think about it," I say. "I'm serious." I wave goodbye over my shoulder as I go back to my room.

I send Finn a text about when we're all meeting for dinner and check my messages. No texts or missed calls from any friends, but at least my dad sent me a message. I write back about my day and attach a few pictures from Oxford Street and tell him to show my sister. She'd be in heaven if she were here.

My family was supposed to come visit during my siblings' spring break, but now it's not happening because of the cost of the flights and my dad not being able to take time off work. I kind of had a feeling all along it wouldn't work out. My dad has to pay for all my flights to and from London for breaks, plus he's busy working and taking care of my brother and sister. I shouldn't feel upset, but I selfishly do.

It's about time to meet everyone for dinner and I notice Finn hasn't texted back. Weird. When I've texted him about dinner before, he's always given some sort of acknowledgment. I lock my door, double-check that it's actually locked, then knock on Finn's door. The advantages to having him live two doors down.

"Finn," I yell. "We're getting dinner."

I wait. Nothing.

"Finn." I check the door handle and it wiggles, meaning it's unlocked. I take a deep breath and turn the doorknob. I let the door creak open just enough to see inside. No acknowledgement. I tiptoe into his room. Finn hasn't outdone himself in decorating his space. For all his complaints about my room, his isn't all *that* much better. A few band posters are tacked on his walls, and a small collection of pictures is by his desk, which is where I find Finn. His head is buried in a textbook, his hand scribbling across a notebook at the speed of light. He's wearing a simple T-shirt and black sweatpants.

"Finn," I say again, only this time closer to him. He jumps as if I shouted his name into his ear with a megaphone.

"Shit, Livy," he says. He picks up his pen from the floor. Ink has left its mark all over his hand, and his curls twist in all the wrong directions.

"I've been yelling your name outside your door. You didn't hear me?"

Finn shakes his head. "Sorry." He flips his notebook to a clean page.

"We're going to dinner," I say. "I'm guessing you didn't see my text either."

"I've been busy," Finn says.

"Come take a break then," I say. "You probably need it."

He shakes his head. "I can't stop." His stomach roars as he continues writing.

"You weren't going to stop for dinner, were you?" He ignores me and keeps writing, which means what I said is true. He just doesn't want to admit it.

"Finn." I place my hand on his shoulder. "Take a quick break to eat. You deserve it."

"Fine," he mumbles in defeat. "Let me change, and I'll meet you in the hall."

A few minutes later, Finn walks out in a black sweater with brushed hair and his tan backpack slung over his shoulder.

"Let's go," he says and walks down the hall with his head down. I have to power walk to even try to keep up with him.

"Are you okay?"

He pretends like he doesn't hear me and pushes open the door of Queen Victoria House. I follow behind, and the cold air chills my bones. I should've brought a warmer jacket.

"How's your day been?" I try. Nothing. Not a word. Okay, so he's not in the mood to talk. I hope he's not mad at me for making him come to dinner. That would make zero sense because he's obviously hungry. If anything, he should be thanking me.

We walk in silence into the caf, and I'm greeted by instrumental Christmas music and what smells like roasted chicken. Twinkle lights shine in every window, and if I close my eyes, it's almost like I've been transported to some fantasy world. Knives scrape against plates and there's the usual chatter of the other students who are there at the same time as us. We grab our food and join the others at our table.

Finn slips into a seat beside me, pulls out his notebook, and throws himself back into his work. *You've got to be kidding me.* I want to yank his hand away and tell him to take a break. His stomach growls so loud I'm sure the entire caf heard it. But no one says a word to him.

Ronan cracks a joke, and everyone laughs. Everyone but Finn. Christmas break starts next week and the general mood of all the students is starting to become more and more relaxed with each finished exam. Once we get through our exams, we get the rest of December off and I'll finally get to go home.

"I don't know what I'm going to do all break without my girl," Ronan says.

"Oh please," Hannah says, lightly punching him. "You'll live. We're only an hour apart."

We launch into a conversation about Christmas traditions and our plans for the break. Finn contributes nothing. His pen scribbles harder into his notebook and it's only a matter of time until he punctures the page.

"Give it a break for a second," I whisper to him and place my hand on his shoulder. He hasn't touched his food, and at this point, it's probably cold.

He shakes his head and keeps scribbling. At least he acknowledged me this time.

"It's Christmas," I offer.

"I'm well aware, thank you."

Equations fill up his page, written in a language that's foreign to me. Physics problems and solutions. He doesn't even have a sheet he's studying from. He writes a random problem down and solves it. Over and over again.

"I think you'll do okay on the exam," I say.

Finn keeps working on the equation and ignores me. Well, I tried. I join back into the conversation with everyone else.

Finn slams his hands on the table, rattling our dishes. "God," he shouts and our conversation comes to a halt midsentence.

"Finn, what the hell's up with you, mate?" Ronan asks. "You've been acting weird all week."

All eyes are on Finn. He takes a deep breath and closes his notebook as if he's just now realized he's been ignoring everyone.

"It's just school," he says. "It's really overwhelming." He picks up his fork with his ink-stained hand. It shakes from writing so much as he takes a bite of his chicken, then glances at me. I didn't realize until now how heavy the bags under his eyes were. It's like I'm sitting next to a zombie.

"It's not worth stressing yourself out," Bailey says, finally breaking the silence. "Finn, you're so smart. You're going to crush your exams."

Finn stares at his plate as if he's fascinated by the design of it. We're all silent, as if we're afraid to talk. Finn finishes the rest of his chicken, then places his notebook in his backpack.

"I'm, erm, going to go back to QVH and have a shower. I'm really exhausted," he says. He gets up and leaves before we can say anything.

"What's up with him?" Hannah says once Finn's out of sight.

I shrug. "He wouldn't talk to me either. I had to practically drag him out of his room."

"Not this again," Bailey says. "Was he studying?"

I nod, and Ronan groans.

"It's ridiculous," he says. "The boy's so smart. Like insanely smart. As in, he could get through school without ever touching a book and still make perfect marks. The most intelligent person I've ever met. He can explain anything and spit out facts about everything." Ronan shakes his head. "But he's constantly studying to the point of exhaustion. It's so weird. Finals time last year, I'm positive he never would've stopped to eat or sleep if we didn't make him."

I'd forgotten Ronan was Finn's neighbor last year. And that everyone else knew each other and that whatever was happening with Finn, they'd experienced before. This wasn't anything new for them.

"Is he okay?" I ask.

Ronan nods as he stuffs another bite of mashed potatoes into his mouth. "Yeah, don't worry about him. He's fine. He just has his moments of extreme studying, where it almost consumes him. I don't know why. But that's why I've been trying to get him to go out more and just have fun. It's good for him to loosen up."

Our conversation shifts back to the upcoming break and our exciting plans. Eventually, the evening runs its course and a warm shower is calling my name, so I excuse myself from the table. As I walk back to Queen Victoria House by myself, I count two windows down from mine to find Finn's. It's dark, and I breathe a sigh of relief. Either he's done studying and has gone to bed, left his room to go somewhere, or he's studying in the dark. I'm choosing to believe the first one.

But as I climb Queen Victoria House's steep drive, I find the answer to Finn's whereabouts. He's sitting on the low wall that surrounds the front grounds, clutching his phone to his ear with one hand and using the other to hold his head.

"Please, Georgia," he cries out. "You can't do this to me."

I'm definitely not supposed to be hearing this conversation, but I don't want to walk past Finn while he's mid-conversation. So I do the only logical thing and crouch behind a nearby bush. I won't eavesdrop. I'll just wait until Finn's off the phone and back inside before I go in.

Although, Finn's talking a little too loud that it's making it hard *not* to eavesdrop.

"I did everything for you," he says. "I did everything you wanted, and it still wasn't good enough. I don't know what else you want from me, but I'll do anything. Please don't leave me alone at Christmas. I need you. You know that."

His voice breaks, and even though I can't see Finn's face now, I imagine he's probably trying his hardest to hold it together. There's silence, and I wish I could hear what Georgia's saying to him.

"Georgia." It comes out in a sob. Finn's breath is heavy, and I picture his entire body trembling as I hear him cry. It takes everything in me not to abandon my hiding place and run out to him. His footsteps stomp up the three steps, and Queen Victoria House's door slams behind him.

I count to thirty, then make my way inside. I don't even allow myself to think before I knock on Finn's door. I can't not do anything when I know my best friend's hurting.

"It's me," I add for good measure.

Finn cracks the door open just enough to pop his head out. His eyes are red as he wipes a tear away. "Really poor timing, Olivia," he says.

"Is everything okay?" I ask, even though I very clearly know my answer.

"Georgia broke up with me," he forces out.

"Do you need to talk? Is there anything I can do?"

He shakes his head. "I just want to be alone right now, alright? I'll see you tomorrow."

My heart breaks leaving Finn to feel upset by himself,

but I have to respect what he wants. "Call me if you need me," I say. "I'm always here for you."

Finn gives me a tight nod, then retreats back into his room. As much as I want Finn's relationship issues to work out for his sake, I hate Georgia in this moment for breaking his heart. I hate the pain he's feeling on just the other side of the door. But I have to give him his space and hope he heals.

11

It's our last class of Walking History before winter break and Finn and I are walking along the streets of South Kensington trying to find some of our final sites for this semester. Rows of towering, identical houses line the streets, and a woman bundled up in a black coat with a scarf tossed over her shoulder strolls past us as she walks her little white dog. Finn's been silent the whole time. His under eyes are still dark and he's wearing the same black sweater from yesterday.

"I'm sorry about last night," Finn says, finally breaking the silence between us. "I didn't want you to have to see me like that."

"It's okay, Finn," I assure him. "How're you doing today?"

He gives me a small shrug. "Actually, better than I expected, I guess. I don't know. It never feels great to get broken up with. Even though I'd been questioning our

130

relationship lately and whether I was still happy with her, it was a bit of a shock. It's just hard this time of year with everything going on."

"Dealing with a breakup and worrying about finals has got to be a lot."

Finn lets out a long exhale. "Sorry about dinner too. I didn't mean to be so tense."

"So you're not mad at me for barging in and dragging you out of your room?"

Finn gives me a tight smile. "I needed to be dragged out of my room, Livy."

"Seriously though, I know you're going to crush the physics exam," I say. Last night's conversation with Ronan repeats in my mind. "Don't let it stress you out. I mean, easier said than done, I'm sure, but still. Ronan was saying that you're really, really smart. I'm sure you're going to be fine."

I'd seen his intelligence. I'd seen it from the very first day when he knew all the answers to the clues. I'd seen it during our time doing homework together in my room. He could solve almost any problem without it giving him trouble, and he never stopped until he got the right answer. Exams should be the least of his concerns.

"It's not school," Finn whispers. "School's easy. It's the holidays." He sighs and his breath forms a cloud in the London cold. "I really don't want to spend Christmas in Liverpool. But I imagine you're excited to go back to the States, aren't you?"

My dad bought my plane ticket a month ago, and last

night, he called to go over the details. In a short amount of time, I'd be back with my family and friends. Christmas is one of my favorite times of the year. During Christmas, everything's happy and perfect. Everyone's in a good mood, and the streets of downtown Bartonsville are dotted with lights. We all gather downtown for the Christmas parade and Duke's starts selling homemade gingerbread and their specialty peppermint hot chocolate. I don't ever remember a time when we didn't put aside our busy schedules to gather as a family to stake out the best view for the parade. There was even a time when Emily and I got to ride on a float her mom's friend's business put on. That was the definition of pure childhood magic.

"I can't wait to have my old life back," I say.

"Sure, whatever's still there," Finn says.

"Stop trying to burst my bubble. There's so much I'll be able to do at home that I can't do here. Like, going to holiday parties with Emily and Ryan. Driving around and looking at lights with my family. Painting with all my favorite art supplies. Going to Duke's for their homemade Christmas cookies."

Finn stops, and I almost bump into him.

"Turn around," he says. "Let me take you to get the best dessert you've ever had."

"I'm pretty sure nothing can beat Duke's," I say, then proceed to tell Finn about the diner and how Sandy always has the case stocked full of fresh cookies, cakes, and pies that change with the seasons.

"Well, Livy," Finn says. "I guess you'll just have to try my place and see for yourself."

We walk for about ten minutes until we reach a little shop on the corner of the street that's pastel-pink with a whole garden of flowers around the door. Flowers cover the pink walls inside, and delicate little cakes and pastries sit behind the glass. I've never seen such beautiful cakes in my life. The icing coats the cakes like fresh fallen snow, and the tiniest flowers fill the corners. They have every flavor imaginable. Rose, lavender vanilla, lemon cream, chocolate raspberry, strawberry blossom. It's an overwhelming decision.

"This was my mum's favorite place," Finn says. "We came here all the time when I lived in London." He points to a little, square pink cake labeled chocolate raspberry. "That's my favorite."

"That's the one I want to try, then," I say.

At the register, I dig out my wallet from my purse, but Finn stops me.

"I've got it," he says.

"Finn," I protest as he hands the cashier his credit card.

"Happy early Christmas," he says as we carry our plates over to a table. "Now here's one thing you can get in London, but not in Massachusetts."

I bite into my little chocolate cake, and it's heavenly. The raspberry glaze compliments the rich chocolate. I've never tasted a cake this moist in my life. Finn's right. I can't get something this good anywhere in Massachusetts. Even Sandy's desserts don't compare to this cake.

"Mmm," I say through my mouthful. "Thank you, Finn."

I'm shoving my cake in my mouth like my life depends on it while Finn's cutting off dainty bites as if he wants it to last forever.

"The last time I was here was before I moved," he says.

"This place is the best." I imagine my sister Charlotte sitting here with me and how much she would enjoy it. We always bake during the holidays. Gingerbread, snickerdoodles, yellow cake, any recipe we could get our hands on.

"Aren't you at least excited to be back with your family for the holidays?" I ask. "It might help to take your mind off of Georgia."

He bites at his lip. "My dad and I just don't get on very well. That's all." He takes a sip of his coffee, which came in a darling pale pink cup. He sets it down and traces his finger along the handle. "It's kind of weird now."

"Things are a little weird with my family too," I find myself saying. I never usually open up about my family, but I think if anyone could understand, it might be Finn. "It's just me, my dad, my sister, and my brother. My mom left us shortly after my brother was born and never came back. She reconnected with someone from college, divorced my dad, and gave him full custody."

"Oh?" Finn raises his eyebrows. "Do you have much communication with her?"

"I haven't talked to her since she left, which was when I was little. It's weird because it's like she was never there since she left when I was so young. She worked a lot when I was young, but then she started traveling for work. I guess along the way, she was traveling to see John, her now husband. It's like she was already gradually fading out of our lives. I remember asking my dad when she was coming home. 'In a week,' he'd say. Only then, a week would pass. And another week. And then eventually, she just never came home."

I don't remember much about her, and that might be a bad thing, but it's not like she ever reached out to us. She wouldn't even recognize me if I showed up at her house. I did look her up once, just out of curiosity. She's out in Chicago with her new husband and young daughter. My heart twisted when I clicked through the pictures on her profile. I wish I'd continued living in that "ignorance is bliss" mindset.

"So it's always just been me, my dad, and my siblings. And being away from them for this long has been hard. That's why I'm glad to be going home. To have everything complete again, as much as it can be."

Finn fiddles with his coffee cup again, his eyes focusing on the cup's handle as if he's trying to memorize the design of it.

"Sorry for spilling everything from my life on you," I say. I don't normally tell people all that because no one seems to understand. Their faces always fall and they offer me a sympathetic smile, like they feel bad for me growing up without a mom. But I wouldn't want it any other way. My dad has never once complained, and he's happy. He says all the time that there's no way his life could get any better. He's content with our family and living in Bartonsville.

Finn takes a sip of coffee and relaxes in his seat. "My mum died when I was sixteen."

My heart drops all the way from my chest to the very pit of my stomach. "Oh my god. Finn."

He takes a deep breath. "That's why we really moved to Liverpool. It wasn't because of my dad's job. It was because he couldn't stand to be in London anymore. My parents had been fighting and were already planning to separate. Then, my mum got the cancer diagnosis when I was fourteen. Two years later, she was gone."

His voice shakes, but he keeps going. "My sister was living in Germany for uni at the time, and she's living out there now. So it was just my dad and I left in London. He went and bought a houseboat in Liverpool that barely had enough room for one person and dragged me with him without giving me a say in the matter. It's where he wanted to go when they separated. But then with the diagnosis…"

He takes his glasses off and rubs his eyes. "He still loved my mum even if they'd fallen out of love. Or so he said. They'd been fighting for years leading up to the diagnosis, but he stayed with her. Anyway, after she died, he followed his dreams. I spent two years in Liverpool sleeping on a sofa bed in the living room." He looks down at his lap. "It's all a weird situation now that everything's changed."

All this time, I'd never thought about my dad. He'd do anything for me. What was it like at home with his wife gone forever and his oldest daughter an ocean away? Was it all a weird situation for him now, or was he handling it okay?

"Is that why you aren't exactly looking forward to going home?" I guess.

He nods. "Exactly. Living in Liverpool for two years on a narrow houseboat with just my dad was absolute hell. That's why I desperately wanted to come back to London because, at the end of the day, this city's home. I didn't want to run and escape like my dad did. But when I came back, nothing was the same. My family was gone, our house had been sold, all my friends had gone all over for uni, and the city I'd once loved suddenly felt incredibly lonely. Georgia was the only one I had left. It seemed like she was the only one still here who knew what I'd gone through. And now, she's gone too."

Instinct rushes over me and I reach for Finn's hand across the table and give it a squeeze. He lifts his eyes up to meet mine.

"You're so incredibly strong, Finn." I can't imagine the heartbreak of losing your mother as a teenager, then having your entire life uprooted when all you wanted was for everything to stay the same. And now, losing his girl-friend, who he'd thought was his only support here.

He purses his lips and shakes his head. "I still have a hard time here on certain days. Little things will suddenly remind me of my mum and I just lose it. I can't even help it." He pauses. "I've never really told anyone all this before."

"I'm glad you told me," I say. "You're the only one I've met here who seems to understand that change is hard." As much as he annoyed me in the beginning, it's true. He's the only one I can truly relate to.

"I like that we can talk about real things, and I can trust you," Finn says. "I'm glad Mike partnered us together. It's like he knew we needed each other. Maybe I'm not so alone now without Georgia."

"You're not alone at all. Whether you know it or not, there are so many people here who support you and want the best for you."

"But I don't want to put that weight on everyone else," he says. "I never feel comfortable telling anyone about my mum. No one here really knows. It's one of those things where once you tell people, I feel like they look at and treat you differently. I just don't want to go about like that. I'd rather keep everything in and deal with it on my own."

"I mean, I'm not quick to tell anyone that my mom up and left," I say. "It's the same sort of thing."

"I just don't want anyone to see me as broken," Finn mutters. "Georgia had already seen me at my worst, so she knew how broken I was. She told me no one would ever be able to handle all my baggage in the way she could."

"First off, that's not true at all. And secondly, you're not broken, Finn. I think everyone can see all the good in you, even if you try to hide it. Like Nicola, for example," I say, remembering something from the beginning of the semester. "That time I accidentally skipped, she mentioned to me that you were one of her best writers, that you were full of emotion. I never told you that."

The corner of his lips turns into the smallest fraction of a smile. "I'm not *that* good of a writer. But that was the only time I felt like I could fully express what I was feeling. She was the only professor I told that my mum had died. She was the one who told Mike. Because normally if you fail a class here, you go on academic probation. But I literally couldn't bear to go out in the city and visit sites that still reminded me so much of my mum. So that's why I failed. I could barely get myself to leave the room. I skipped days of class."

He takes another sip of coffee. "It hurts to know I failed a class too. I feel like I've let my mum down and myself. But after Mike found out what was going on, he decided to give me another chance. So, as long as I pass this time around, I won't be on probation."

We finish our coffees and our cakes and Finn tells me more about his mom and growing up in London. His hazel eyes glisten behind his glasses, bright and full. To imagine what those eyes have seen and the pain they've hidden. It'd never even occurred to me to think about what my dad might have felt when my mom left him for a different lover. Not that it's the same situation, but he must have been hurt, even if now he says he's happier without her.

"After she died," Finn says. "Nothing was ever the same. Not my family, my life, my hometown. Even coming back to London feels different." He shakes his head. "Everything changed before I had time to realize what was happening."

"I'm glad I met you," I say. "You understand how changes that happen out of your control can absolutely suck. I'm so thankful for our friendship."

Finn takes our little china plates to the counter. "You understand things," he says. "You're one of the few."

12

On the last night of the semester before break, Queen Victoria House is abuzz with excitement. Everyone has finished their exams, and their train and plane tickets are booked. Tomorrow, I'll be landing at the Boston Logan International Airport with my family ready to pick me up. I'll finally get to see Emily and Ryan in person. This time, I'm finally going to tell Ryan how I feel. I don't want to waste any more time.

I see the scene unfolding in my mind. The three of us will hang out, but Emily will be late like she always is because she forgot her lipstick or something like that. It'll just be me and Ryan, and finally I'll have the courage to tell him how I feel. His face will melt into a smile, and he'll hug me and tell me he feels the same. It'll all be worth the wait.

But for now, I've got one more night here in London.

Hannah, Bailey, and Ronan are all getting ready to go out to some ice bar club that's serving spiked hot chocolate. As much as I wanted to go with them, I'd been putting off packing all week because of exams. Plus, I don't want to be out late since my flight is early in the morning. Dad drilled it in my head to get to the airport at least three hours early because one time he missed a flight and had to spend the night in the airport. I'm not spending another night here, especially if it's going to be on an airport floor.

My friends invited Finn to go out, too, but he said he had to talk to his dad for a while about their plans for the break. Ever since the afternoon in the bakery, he's been better. He's still tense about everything and studied up until the very minute of his exams, but it makes sense now. Of course the holidays would be a hard time.

I pull out my suitcase, which hasn't left the corner of my room since the first week of school and open my closet. I don't think I'll need to take every sweater I own home. I'm debating between a black and dark gray sweater, then end up throwing them both in the bag. One extra sweater won't take up that much space, and it'll be good to have options.

A singular knock on the door startles me since most people are either out or busy packing. When I open the door, I find Finn there, completely bundled up with a brown coat, scarf, and a red beanie like he's about to trek across Antarctica, but in a fashionable way. Of course he could make trekking in Antarctica attractive.

He glances over my shoulder into my room. "Are you really going to spend your last night in London packing?"

"Well, yeah. That's the plan." I make a mental note to gather up my toiletries tonight to make things easier in the morning. I also needed to set aside a spare outfit for my carry-on in case they lose my luggage or something goes wrong.

Finn shakes his head. "Leave it to you, Livy." He reaches out his hand. "Come on. Let's go out and do something fun instead."

"I can't. I seriously have to pack. My flight's early."

"Livy. It's Christmas time in London and you're in your room, alone, packing. I simply won't allow it. You've got to celebrate." He throws his arms up.

I can't help laughing. "Says the guy who is the most serious about school. Having fun? Celebrating? What's that?"

"Hey now, I can have fun if I want to. Plus, exams are over now. Since we won't see each other for the actual holidays, we need to celebrate now while we're together. I'll help you pack when we get back. I promise."

Finn smiles, a true, genuine smile. One that's so rare I want to grab my phone and capture a picture of it before it disappears. I want to swim in his left dimple, and the twinkle in his hazel eyes puts all the stars to shame. But then, images of Ryan fill my head. The way Ryan would smile when I'd bring a batch of my chai spice cookies to school on a fall day. Or the way his face would light up when he'd talk about *Star Wars*. It's Ryan who's waiting for me at home. It's Ryan who'll be in Boston for the next three years of school with me. Not Finn. Finn is just my friend. And there's nothing wrong with hanging out with a friend. I kick my half-empty suitcase aside, grab my coat off my bed, and follow Finn down the hall and out of Queen Victoria House.

We take the Tube to Hyde Park, where a section has been transformed into a winter wonderland. I've been to this park in the daylight for class, but it's like I'm in a different part of London. Vendors cluster, selling holiday crafts or assorted sweets. Rides have been set up seemingly overnight and children dart between us to get in line.

And lights. There are lights everywhere. Giant snowflakes illuminate our path as we walk farther into the park. I'm no longer in London but in some magical fantasy world. An ice-skating rink sits in the midst of it all with a canopy of Christmas lights like falling snow. Finn points to it.

"That's where we're going first," he says.

"Oh no." I shake my head. "I'm not doing that. I'll fall and crack my head open, then I'll never get to go home."

Finn tugs at my arm and practically drags me over to the rink, where he asks for two tickets.

"I can pay for myself," I say.

Finn pretends not to hear me as he hands over his card. "Consider it a Christmas gift from me," he whispers as we grab our skates and walk over to a bench.

"Thank you."

"By the way, I'm rubbish at ice skating too," he says as we're lacing up our skates.

"Oh, now you tell me. That's reassuring."

He shrugs. "At least if we fall, we'll both end up in hospital."

"If that happens, you're paying my hospital bill," I say, pointing my finger at him. "And reimbursing my dad for my plane ticket."

"Come on, Livy, live a little." We step onto the ice and we're both gripping the railing as if our lives depend on it. "But if you get hurt, I'll pay for everything," he whispers.

Twinkle lights shine above us, and the neon lights from the roller coasters engulf us. Men and women skate past us hand in hand. Even a little girl skates past us as if she's grown up on skates. Meanwhile, Finn and I have moved about one inch from where we started. My knuckles are white as snow from gripping the railing. I slide my right foot forward and wobble as I regain my balance.

"How are these people so good? Is ice skating some sort of requirement you have to learn in school here?" I say as more people skate past us. Not a single person is struggling, and they're all acting as if ice skating's as easy as walking down the street.

"If it is, I completely missed that lesson," Finn says. We slide another inch. "This is rubbish. I'm going for it."

Finn pushes off the railing and glides across the ice

like a baby learning to walk. His arms are outstretched for balance.

"It's not so bad," he says as he wobbles. "You've just got to find your balance."

"You're doing great," I say. I'm still clinging to the railing for dear life.

Finn laughs and takes another step forward. Then he completely wipes out.

"Finn! Are you okay?"

A child skates right past him, and Finn bursts out laughing. "My arse," he moans. "Ow!" He grips the wall and pushes himself back up. "I'm not giving up quite yet."

Finn holds on to the rail for a few steps before he pushes himself off again.

"Okay, Finn, balance," I say. His whole body wavers until he steadies himself and takes a few careful steps. "You've got this."

He glides alongside me for a couple more steps, then reaches for my left hand, which will probably need to be pried off the railing. "Come on, Livy," he says.

I shake my head. "If one of us goes down, then both of us are going down."

He puts his hands on his hips. "I've got my balance figured out now." He shoots me another one of his smiles. "Trust me." He offers his hand out to me again. "I'll help you balance?"

I surrender myself to Finn and let him take hold of

my hand. His gloved hand interlaces my bare one, and all the fears I had about ice skating vanish into the air. With Finn here, nothing in the world can stop us.

We're nothing like the couples who glide past us. We grip each other's hand with full force. My hand goes numb after a minute, but I'm not about to let go of Finn's hand. We're the shakiest ones on the ice, but I don't care. The lights above us shine like stars and an instrumental of "We Wish You a Merry Christmas" plays in the distance. It's easy to forget that we're surrounded by people.

In this moment, nothing else seems to matter. As my skates glide over the ice, I find myself wishing I could let go of Finn's hand and spin and twirl across the rink. Being out in this winter wonderland during my favorite time of the year has activated all my Christmas joy. How strange that only a few hours ago, I'd been counting down the minutes until I could be back in Bartonsville with my family and Emily and Ryan, and now I wanted to capture this moment in time and live in it for just a little bit longer. This time next year, I wouldn't be in London for Christmas. This wouldn't be my life anymore. Maybe I can soak this all in and enjoy it while I have it.

After about twenty minutes, we make it around one lap without falling. Finn puffs a sigh of relief, and his breath clouds in front of him. His hand lingers in mine, even though we've made it back to the exit.

"I was a little worried there, I'll admit," he says.

"Shall we do some rides instead? A different kind of thrill?"

Again, Finn pays for my ticket despite my protest, and we ride tons of the rides in the park. These aren't little rides that would pop up at our county fair at home. It's as if an entire amusement park was plucked off the ground and dropped in Hyde Park. Towering roller coasters with plunging drops and electric lights crowd the park.

We save the biggest roller coaster for last. As we secure our seat belts, my heart starts to pound. It's been a while since I've ridden a roller coaster, let alone one with this many drops and loops.

"Ready, Livy?" Finn says.

"Ready as I'll ever be," I say.

The roller coaster lurches forward and climbs up, up, up until all the lights of the rides in Hyde Park and the London skyline dazzle below us. Then we're soaring down. Finn's hand is in mine, and I don't know if I grabbed it first or if he did, but I don't let go. We approach the first loop, and Finn's screaming drowns out all Christmas cheer in the park. Another loop, another loop, another loop, and I'm screaming too and squeezing Finn's hand. Before I know it, the ride is slowing down. It's over.

The ride stops, and I'm holding Finn's hand still. *Why is his hand still in mine?* The people in front of us lift off their seat belts. I let go of Finn's hand like it's suddenly burning coals in my hand and jump out of the ride a little too quickly.

"Okay," I say with way too much enthusiasm. "Let's go."

"That was amazing," Finn says as we exit the ride. He has a huge grin on his face that hasn't disappeared all night, and it's like I'm seeing another side of him. No longer is he the physics-obsessed boy who never stops working. I know now why Ronan wanted him to get out and let loose. And tonight, I have him all to myself.

"You know, I never would've thought you'd be some adrenaline junky," I say.

"I'm not one to seek it out, but this is the only time it's acceptable to scream out your frustration about the holidays and have no one judge you."

I lightly punch his shoulder. "Oh, please."

There's one ride we've been saving for last: The Wheel. The huge Ferris wheel promises to give riders breathtaking views of the city. I zip my jacket up all the way as we make our way over. The temperature has fallen even more as the night's gone on.

"Are you chilly?" Finn says. "I'll get us some hot chocolate."

"No, it's totally okay," I say. Plus, I didn't want to think about how much Finn had already spent tonight.

"Livy." Finn tilts his head and puts his hands on his hips. "What's Christmas without hot chocolate?"

"You do have a point." I hand him my credit card, but he shakes his head.

"This night is all my treat," he says as he heads over to a hot chocolate stand.

With our hot chocolate in hand, we join the line for the wheel. Before long, we're climbing into our pod to begin our journey. Up above, London shines. The dots of lights from the buildings decorate the skyline. It's like magic seeing the whole city spread out in front of us. It's the most perfect way to end the night. My hot chocolate warms my body while the neon lights of the rides below us twinkle like rainbow-colored stars.

"Maybe I'll miss London just a little bit," I finally say.

"If this is all it took, I would've taken you to the top of a building sooner," Finn says.

I shake my head. "It wouldn't have been the same. Something about this night has been magical."

Finn turns his head away from me to hide his smile. "Magical. I like that."

We sit in silence as we finish our hot chocolate. It's a comfortable silence; there are no words we can say to fill in for the beauty of the night. I glance over, and I swear Finn's staring at me. His eyes dart away as he takes another sip of his cocoa. But it doesn't take long for our eyes to meet again for a moment.

"Erm," he says. He glances at his watch as we begin to make our descent. "We better get going after this. It's getting late. And you have your flight tomorrow. I'm still keeping my promise to help you pack."

I take one final glance at London. It's hard to believe it'll be a new year when I come back. It's weird how a place so far away has begun to feel like home. I can't believe I'm actually feeling sad about leaving.

"Thank you, Finn," I say. *Thank you for paying for the ice skating and the rides and the hot chocolate and for making my last night here so magical and for making me feel really, really happy* is what I actually want to say, but all I can manage to get out is, "Thank you so much for everything."

———

When we get back, the halls of Queen Victoria House are quiet. Many lights are off, and no one's roaming the halls to visit a friend. A lot of people who live locally have already gone home.

I unlock my door and find my black suitcase sitting there where I left it, completely barren and abandoned. I groan as I sit down beside it.

"Alright," Finn says, staring into my closet. "I intend to keep my promise. Tell me what you want me to put in there, and I'll fold it all up nicely."

"That blue sweater, two jeans, two leggings, my sweatshirt." I point to a few things hanging in my closet.

"I've never seen you wear this." Finn pulls out a rose-colored sweater with little silver sparkles on it.

"I don't know why I even brought that," I say. "You can put it in the suitcase. I never wear it, so I might as well take it home."

"You should wear it," Finn says. "It'd look pretty on you." He folds it and places it in the suitcase.

Did Finn indirectly call me pretty? Or did he just like

that sweater? I haven't even worn it since I was a sophomore in high school.

"Anything else?" Finn says.

"Well, just my toiletries and stuff. I'll just get that after…" *After you go.* But I couldn't bring myself to say it.

Finn adjusts his glasses. "Livy," he says. "This has been the best night of my life. I don't think I've been this happy…really since before…before my mum died."

He closes my closet and zips my suitcase. His work is done, but he lingers by my closet. "I don't want this night to end," he says. "Can I, erm, stay for a bit longer?"

"Um, sure," I say. I did need to get to sleep soon, but I let Finn wrap himself in my blanket and get comfortable on my bed.

"Well," Finn says. "You're set. It'll be weird not seeing you around."

"But you're going back to Liverpool tomorrow, right?"

Finn shakes his head. "No. There's not enough room on the houseboat. I always feel like I'm crowding up my dad's space. I'm going to stay here and just go up for Christmas Eve through New Year's. Plus, my sister will be there with him. They get on much better than we do."

I join him on my bed. "But you won't have anyone here," I say. "Won't you be lonely?" I can't imagine how awful it'd be to stay in Queen Victoria House all alone during the holidays.

Finn shrugs. "I'll make do. I'm better off staying in London. Better than going to bloody Liverpool. It's not home. And it's definitely not home without my mum. We were always so close, whereas my sister Amy has always been closer with my dad. So it's weird now going back."

"It's kind of weird for me to be going home too," I finally admit. "I've got my whole life there, but it's different. I hardly ever talk to Emily and Ryan now. It's like they don't need me anymore. Like, did I even matter to them if they could move on so easily?"

"No, people are just like that," Finn says. "Change happens, then they don't know how to act. After I moved, my best friends didn't talk to me. They were the ones I needed the most and, once I was gone, their life kept on going without me."

That was it. Emily and Ryan's lives had kept going, whether I was there or not. Just like my life kept going in London even though I was thrown into it. I'd made friends and had a whole new life here that didn't involve Emily and Ryan. It wouldn't be the same if they were here. But once I saw them again, things would fall back into place. We'd been inseparable for years. They wouldn't forget me.

But I don't want to think about that right now.

"Going home just for Christmas feels strange," I say. "Because it's temporary, only to visit. I know I'm eventually going to have to come back here at the end of break."

"Home for the holidays," Finn says. "Welcome to the real world."

I yawn and click my phone on. It's almost midnight, and I've got to be up and ready to go by seven. "I think I might get ready for bed. I didn't realize it was so late," I say.

Finn nods and tosses my blanket back on my bed. I follow him to my door, then wait as he lingers there for just a second too long. "Can I see you again in the morning? Before you go?"

I nod and tell him what time I'm leaving. Finn fiddles with his glasses, adjusting them so they sit just right.

"Thanks for the best night ever," he says and pulls me in for a hug. As his arms embrace me, warmth from his body radiates into mine. He lets go and opens my door. "Goodnight, Livy. I'll see you in the morning."

I set my alarm and throw myself into bed, praying sleep comes quick and fast so I'm not completely exhausted in the morning. My head hits the pillow, and I pull my blanket around me. The lingering scent of his cologne is all I can focus on, cedarwood with a hint of vanilla, and before I can even try to stop them, thoughts of Finn fill my head. Like his wool-gloved hand interlaced in mine during all the big drops of the roller coasters. The way his tortoise glasses accented his eyes. His dimples when he smiled under the twinkle lights. Thoughts of Finn crash and bump into each other in my mind, fighting for superiority.

I close my eyes tighter in an effort to squeeze all of my thoughts of Finn out of me. Instead, I try to think of everything that makes me happy, just like my dad always told me to do when I was young and would have a nightmare. Painting. Warm cookies. Flower gardens. Walking the streets of London with Finn.

My eyes shoot open. What am I doing? I reach for my phone, download a white noise app, and turn the volume all the way up. I let the sound drown out all my thoughts until I can feel myself start to surrender to sleep.

My alarm's happy chime plays on my phone after what feels like ten minutes since I'd fallen asleep. I groan as I turn it off and stretch my arms. Normally, I'm quick to get out of bed in the mornings. But today, I want to snooze my alarm for another two hours. The sunlight floods into my room, making it impossible to fall back asleep even if I wanted to. If I'm lucky, I'll be able to take a nap on the plane. By tonight, I'll be back in Massachusetts and finally in my own bed.

I toss back my covers. Better to just get up and get it over with. I gather up my suitcase and change into the outfit I laid out the night before. I step out into the hallway and lock my door for the last time this semester. Right as I do so, Finn steps out of his room, yawning.

"Good morning," he says and yawns again. His curls are a mess, but even if they're going in all the wrong directions, I still want to run my fingers through them. And he has his sweatpants on.

My heart beats at a hundred beats per second. There's something about seeing him so vulnerable and still half asleep. This is what Georgia would see when he'd spend the night at her place. I can't imagine what it's like waking up beside him.

"Right, Livy, I'm pretty useless in the mornings, but I'll help you get on your way. Massachusetts awaits," Finn says. He carries my suitcase out and down the drive. He sets it down and stuffs his hands in his pockets. If only he could follow me all the way to the airport and get on the plane with me.

"Well," I say. "I guess this is goodbye until next year."

"Bye until next year," Finn says. "Let me know when you get in, will you?"

"Of course," I say. "I'll be in touch. I hope you're not too lonely here."

Finn shrugs. "I'll be fine. Enjoy the holidays at home with your family and friends."

"You too. I mean, have a good Christmas with your dad and sister. Try to have a little bit of fun."

Finn gives me a tight nod.

I glance at the time on my phone. "I should probably get going. My dad told me to get to the airport three hours early to make sure I have enough time to get through and all that."

I should go, but I can't get my feet to move. I'm glued

to Queen Victoria House's driveway, unwilling to leave Finn behind for the next three weeks.

"Right," Finn says. He pulls me in for a quick hug, and I pray he can't feel the speed at which my heart's beating.

"Have a safe flight, and do call, please," he says.

"I will."

With one final glance at Queen Victoria House and Finn, I'm off on my way to Heathrow. I'm glad the Tube stop isn't too far away because the December chill is brutal this morning. The Tube ride takes forever from North London to the airport. Bailey warned me it would be a good hour, at least. I put in my earbuds and count down how many stops I have left.

I'm glad Dad told me to leave early because by the time I make it to Heathrow, it's tight. It seems like I have to wait for ages to check my bag. And of course, with my luck, my gate's the very last one in the terminal. I refuse to be one of those people who runs through the airport, but it's going to be close. I'll power walk. That seems a little more normal. By the time I reach the gate and sit down, they're already calling boarding groups.

I've got a window seat beside an older British couple. Maybe they're going to Boston for a getaway. Or maybe they have family there. Or maybe it's been a lifelong dream of theirs to visit Boston. Or Boston might not even be their final destination. Maybe they only have a layover there.

I breathe a sigh of relief as I settle into my seat. I

made it onto my flight and I'm finally getting to go home. I did it all on my own. But the wave of relief I expect to flood over me doesn't come. I stare out the window as the plane lifts off the ground, and soon, England is miles below us. I'd been counting down to the day I'd get to leave for break, but now my heart aches for another place that has come to feel like home.

We're 35,000 feet up, and I'm thinking about him. Finn's smile shone brighter than any of the lights last night. I can't get that image out of my mind. But it was nothing more than him feeling bad for me because it was the end of the semester, and I was spending it alone. It was just Finn being my partner from history class, looking out for me and trying to boost my spirits. He was only my friend trying to make me feel happy before I went home and helping me enjoy Christmas in London.

I wish I could call him right now. I sink down in my seat. I'm going to see Ryan in less than twenty-four hours. But I didn't want to see Ryan. I wanted to see Finn.

I flip my tray table down and drop my head into my hands. Why was I even thinking about Finn like this when this whole semester I've been holding out for Ryan? Finn's been nothing more than a good friend to me. And anyway, the semester's halfway over. I'm sure once I see Ryan, all these stupid feelings for Finn will evaporate. I've just been away from Ryan for a while. It'll be fine.

Five hours are left until we land, and my head's going to explode. I can't call or text anyone, and no one else knows about my situation. The woman beside me is asleep with her head on her husband's shoulder. Would that have been me and Finn if we were on the plane together? I shove the thought out of my head. I shouldn't be imagining things like that. Not when there's Ryan. I'm sure Finn's probably not going crazy thinking about me right now. I'm the last thing on his mind, I'm sure. I was probably just overthinking this whole situation. We had fun together last night as friends, and there's nothing more to it. I couldn't let there be anything more to it. Falling in love with my British Walking History partner definitely wasn't a part of my college plan.

———

Somehow, I must have managed to fall asleep because I'm startled by the captain's voice over the speaker.

"Ladies and gentlemen, we're approaching Boston Logan International Airport. The local time is 2:05 P.M. and the weather's looking a bit chilly—thirty-seven degrees. Flight attendants, prepare for landing."

Once we land, I wait for my luggage in the baggage claim. When I finally get service, I send Finn a quick text to let him know I landed. He responds a few minutes later:

> Good. I was waiting to hear from you.
> Have a happy holiday.

My dad has sent me a bunch of texts letting me know

exactly where he is and that he's been tracking my flight and knows that I've landed. Translation: *Where are you?*

I take a deep breath and walk down the hallway to the airport's main entrance. It's not that I don't want to see my family. I do, but not this instant. I need time to clear my head of jet lag and Finn. I can't think about him right now. No one here even knows who he is. I haven't told my family or my friends anything about him. They don't even know he exists. I can't throw that on them now. *Hi Dad, guess what? I met a British boy over in London, and I can't stop thinking about him as more than a friend.* That wouldn't go over well.

"Olivia," my dad shouts as he full-on sprints over to me. Charlotte and Lucas trail behind him.

"Hi, Dad," I say as he throws his arms around me, pulling me in so tight I'm afraid I'm not going to be able to breathe.

"Hey, Liv," Charlotte says as I pull her in for a hug next. "I've missed you so much."

"Let's get you back home so we can have our family back together," Dad says.

I follow my family to my dad's car, and we load up my suitcase. I can't stop yawning on the way home. Even with the time difference, it's not even that late in London.

"Did you manage to sleep much on the plane?" Dad asks.

"A little." *But I didn't manage to sleep much last night.* Although I don't want to say that. There was no way I want to explain that I was up until after midnight with a beautiful British boy.

Lucas kicks my seat. "You can't go to bed when we get home," he says. "Charlotte's been putting off baking Christmas cookies until you were home. So you're not going to bed until I get cookies."

I turn around from the front seat and smile at Charlotte. She actually waited for me. A part of me was actually missing. "Thanks, Charlotte," I say.

"It's been hard waiting so long," she says. "I found a few new recipes for us to try. I'm really excited about these snowball cookies."

"Don't forget the crushed peppermint one," Lucas says.

"We'll make whatever cookies you want, Lucas. But I can't promise it'll all happen tonight."

"We still have to go to the store too," Charlotte adds.

"It'll absolutely be worth the wait, though," I say.

As we cruise down the freeway, leaving Boston behind us, home gradually starts to reveal itself to me. I always know we're close to the exit for Bartonsville when I see the faded, wooden billboard for the Wesley Family Farm. It's barely legible at this point since it's been up for as long as I can remember. There have been rumors the farm would be replacing the billboard with a new, modern display, but I hope they never do. The faded billboard is a sign that home's near.

We take the exit for Bartonsville. A stretch of trees lines the road, tall and heavy with the weight of everyone who's come before me. Their bare branches stretch tall and wide, reaching higher into the vast expanse of the blue sky. My cheek lays against the cold of the car's window. I, too, want to reach my arms out like the trees and hold Bartonsville as close to my chest as I can.

Then, as if it's been hidden away only to be newly discovered, the trees give way to Bartonsville's main street. I hold my breath in fear that I'll miss it. The sleepy, colonial buildings are exactly the same as they were when I left them. Duke's comes into view. Marc and Sandy are probably in there right now, chatting with anyone who's wandered in.

We turn down the next street, and I allow myself to settle back in my seat and release a sigh of relief. Bartonsville will never change. No matter how far I go, home will always be here, waiting for me.

My bedroom's a museum of all that I'd left behind: the scrapbook clippings, rainbow paint brushes, and bottles of acrylic paint. I haven't even thought about painting in the past few weeks. I pick up the bottles of paint like I'm studying them for the first time. I can't wait to mix the colors and make my own creation.

I toss myself on my rainbow quilt and send Finn a text:

Made it back home!

Finn's reply comes a moment later:

> Hope you have a nice time. My sister's bloody upset that I'm not coming home until Christmas Eve. Of course my dad takes her side. Let the guilt trip begin.

I stare at his words and wish I could hear him saying them instead of having to read them. I try to imagine his accent saying *bloody*, but it's not the same. I lie back on my bed and close my eyes, imagining what it'd be like if he was here beside me.

He'd walk through my room and pick up the little paint jars and admire the colors. He'd curl up under my quilt and invite me under. I'd feel his hand in mine. I'd take off his glasses, and we'd kiss until we fell asleep…

"Olivia!" My dad's voice brings me out of my trance, thank goodness. Perfect timing on his end. "Dinner's ready."

I run down the stairs because I'm starving. I can't think about Finn like that. I'll only hurt myself if I keep doing it, especially when my freshman year is already half over at this point. Besides, there's Ryan. I needed to think about him instead.

Dad's made a frozen pizza. He even got my favorite brand with the thin crust even though Lucas prefers thick crust and Charlotte hates veggie pizza. On a normal day I'd be thrilled, but I don't want frozen pizza today. It's not going to be anything like this pizza place Finn took me to one day after class. He'd claimed they had the best pizza in the world, besides Italy. And it'd actually been the best pizza I'd ever had in my life. So now I'm scarred from ever enjoying American pizza again.

"Tell me everything," Charlotte says. She picks a pepper off her pizza. "What are your classes like? Have you made a lot of friends? Oh my god, have you run into any of the royals?"

How do I catch my family up on the past semester of my life?

"I don't even know where to start," I say. I fill my family in on my classes and how they're going. I tell them about Bailey, Hannah, and Ronan and how I've finally settled in.

"There's another friend in our group, Finn," I say. "He's my partner in my Walking History class. That class is fun since we get to learn more about London, and it's helped me get to know Finn better too." I tell my family about all the sites we've had to visit for class and everything that I've come to learn about London.

"I'm glad to have you home," my dad says once I've finished updating them. "It's been weird without you here."

After dinner, I take a nice long bath, then go to bed. It feels so good to be back in my own bed, in my own room, in my own house. At least that much hasn't changed. My old routine falls right back into place with my dad making us dinner and me not having to worry so much about taking care of myself on my own. Everything will be okay.

14

Christmas break stretches out in front of me, my return flight to London far out of reach. I zip up my jacket and unlock my car to head to Emily's annual Christmas get-together. It's something she's always hosted since we were in middle school, just me, her, and Ryan watching Christmas movies, eating desserts, and whatever other Christmas activities we feel like doing. It's always been our unofficial start to Christmas break. Emily never fails to have an array of Christmas cookies and we watch a new holiday movie even though it's always predictable, but I like it that way.

I take a deep breath as I walk up the stairs to Emily's house. Butterflies swarm in my stomach even though I have no reason to be nervous. They're my best friends. But it's like I'm about to meet them for the first time and don't know what to expect. I knock twice, and the door immediately flies open.

"Oh my gosh, hi," Emily says when she opens the door. She throws her arms around me. "My honorary British citizen."

Emily's house smells like vanilla cinnamon, the exact candle her mom always has burning. I've missed that smell. I follow Emily into her living room, where there's already a pile of blankets and a tray of cookies. And there he is. Ryan's sitting on the sofa with his feet propped up on the coffee table. Even though he's wearing his tacky Christmas sweater with a giant Rudolph on it, it doesn't matter. He's gotten a haircut and has the smallest amount of stubble. And he's sitting next to a girl I immediately recognize as Maddie.

"Hey," Maddie says. "Nice to meet you in person." *What's she doing here?* This was supposed to be the three of us like old times. A tradition just for Emily, Ryan, and me. There was never anyone else.

"I told Maddie you wouldn't mind if she joined us," Emily says. "She lives in Boston, so it wasn't that far of a drive for her to come down for the night."

"Of course not. No big deal," I say. Except it is kind of a big deal. I hadn't seen my friends since I left for London, and all I wanted was to have a night with them to myself. I didn't want to share them with Maddie. Especially when I don't know her.

I take a seat next to Ryan and grab a blanket from Emily's stack.

"What's up, Olivia?" He flashes me a smile, and I

settle back into the sofa. At least Ryan's still the same. At least he's still happy to see me.

"We should go with *A Special Delivery*," Ryan says. "It's about a mailman who falls in love with the local florist."

Maddie scrunches up her face in disgust. "That sounds incredibly cheesy," she says as she plays with her braid.

That's the whole point of Christmas romances, I want to say. *Of course it's going to be cheesy and predictable, but that's our tradition.*

"We can find something else," Emily offers.

"But Emily, you love cheesy Christmas movies," I remind her.

She shrugs. "Eh, Maddie does have a point. It's always way too obvious how it's going to end. Let's find a comedy or something."

Ryan puts on some sort of Christmas comedy about a family who has every possible thing go wrong during their vacation. I can't even focus on the movie because Emily and Maddie won't stop talking about some guy in their marketing class. I can't believe they're not even paying attention to the movie they wanted to watch.

Maddie whispers something to Emily, and they burst out laughing. I can't help rolling my eyes, then hope they didn't notice. I want to leave right now, go back home, bake cookies with Charlotte, and curl up on the sofa with my family and watch a movie with them. It's like I'm watching what my friendship with Emily was like. Only Maddie's replaced my role. Emily didn't need me.

Ryan's not even paying attention to the movie either. He keeps glancing at his phone and sending a quick text. I notice his phone background is still the same as mine.

"We'll be right back," Emily says as she and Maddie jump up from the couch. "I've got to show Maddie something upstairs."

I reach for the remote on the coffee table. "Do you want me to pause the movie?"

Emily shakes her head. "Nah, you and Ryan can keep watching. Come on, Maddie." They dash up the stairs as anger boils in the pit of my stomach. Everything about this party is an absolute disaster. I hate that everything Finn told me about change and friends is coming true. I can't believe my best friend would move on without me.

But now I'm alone with Ryan. He slips his phone back in his pocket. This is my chance. He hasn't mentioned a girlfriend all night, and I think that would have come up in conversation by now. Emily wouldn't be able to keep that a secret. I'm probably safe to tell him how I feel.

"Ryan," I whisper.

"Yeah?" he says. His blue-gray eyes stare at me with his full attention, like he wants to hear every single word I'm about to tell him. The movie drones on in the background, but neither of us is paying attention to what's going on now.

"I…" Memories of Hyde Park flash through my head: Finn ice skating, Finn's woolen gloves, Finn's glasses reflecting the London skyline. Finn with my blanket wrapped around him, Finn hugging me goodbye in front of Queen Victoria House.

I have Ryan right here, but all I can think about is Finn. It's always been Finn, hasn't it? And even though I can't have Finn, not with only a semester left, I realize it's never been Ryan. I like Ryan, but did I ever love Ryan? Or did I just love the idea of him? We've been apart now for too long that my heart doesn't sing when he says my name, at least not in the way it does when Finn calls me Livy.

I'm no longer clinging to the moments I spent alone with Ryan, moments that were Ryan being a good friend. Then it hits me. Ryan's never given me any hint that he's ever seen me as anything more than a friend. And Finn, well, Finn's complicated. The truth pounds in my heart; the truth I haven't even realized I'd been denying—it's been Finn all along.

I'm absolutely screwed.

"I've missed you, Ryan," is all I can manage to say.

His face melts into a smile. "I've missed you too. It's good to have you home."

Footsteps and a fit of laughter echo from the stairs as Emily and Maddie make their way back to rejoin us, saving me from having to say anything else to Ryan.

"Ryan, Emily showed me that video you were talking about with Steven," Maddie says.

Ryan bursts out laughing. "You didn't."

Ryan dives into the conversation with Maddie and Emily about some guy who I guess he has a class with? I fiddle with a loose thread on my blanket. As if he knows I'm thinking about him, my phone vibrates in my pocket. Grabbing it, I see Finn's name displayed as the caller. I don't even say anything as I walk out onto Emily's back porch and curl up on her outdoor sofa. They probably won't even notice I'm gone.

"Hey, Finn," I say.

"Hello," Finn says. "It's so nice to hear your voice."

"God, it's good to hear yours too." My hand immediately flies to my mouth. I hope that didn't sound desperate. I hope he doesn't think I'm sitting around thinking about him.

"How's your break going? Is it everything you thought it'd be and more?"

"I wish," I say. "I mean, it's so nice being back in my house and in my own bed. And being home with my family. That all feels completely the same as before. But with my friends, it's weird. It's like they've all moved on with their lives, and I don't fit in now. It's almost like they all know I'm temporarily here and soon I'll be gone, then their lives will carry on without me. I miss being in London and going to lunch and getting coffee after class. And I miss taking the Tube everywhere. It's such a pain to have to drive places and sit in traffic and try to find a parking spot. And you know what, I miss British people in general."

Finn chuckles. "Ha. I was right all along."

"Don't take too much victory in it. I'm sure once I

come back home after next semester, everything will fall right back into place."

"Right," Finn says. "I can't believe the year's already half over. We only have a few more months together. It's going to go so fast."

"It'll fly by," I agree. "Before I know it, I'll be back home."

"For good," Finn says.

"Yeah, I'll be home for good," I say. It's weird to think that the next time I make this flight home, I'll be all packed up and leaving London permanently. "How's London with everyone gone?"

"It's fine, I guess. I've had plenty of time to catch up on some reading. Exciting stuff," Finn says. "I've got my train tomorrow. I'm absolutely dreading going to Liverpool. My sister arrived a few days ago, and I know it's going to be absolutely awful. She keeps nagging me about how I'm the reason we can't have a normal Christmas anymore since I'm not staying for very long. And my dad doesn't want to pay for another place for us to go, so we're all going to have to cram into the boat, which means I'm pretty much sleeping in a hallway. It's going to be hell."

The weight of Finn's sigh is so heavy I'm surprised my phone doesn't shatter. "It's never going to be the same," he says. "My dad and I are going to end up fighting the entire time. Then my sister will take his side. And they wonder why I don't want to stay any longer."

"I'm sorry, Finn. That's so hard."

We've texted some since I left, but we haven't talked on the phone until now. In all our conversations, Finn hasn't brought up anything about our night together in Hyde Park. I want to ask him about that night and why he didn't seem to want the night to end. But I don't. Right now doesn't exactly feel like the right moment.

"Anyway," he says. "I'd rather be alone in London than in Liverpool. At least I'm somewhat at home."

I picture Finn in his sweats curled up in his bed reading a book. It's a classic, I bet. Or some sort of physics historical fiction. Once I've allowed my mind to go down the track of theorizing about Finn, I can't stop myself. What does he do when he's all alone in the city? Does he take long walks in the park? Does he stay up late doing physics for fun? Does he sit out at some café sipping his coffee and taking his time?

"How're things going with Ryan?" Finn says, interrupting my thoughts.

"It's good. He's happy to see me," I say. Because he was. And there was no way I was going to admit to Finn that the reason I was unable to tell Ryan I liked him was because I was too busy thinking about being with him instead. "I'm actually over at Emily's for a Christmas party."

"Right," Finn says. "Enjoy your time with them. It's two in the morning here, and I'm absolutely knackered. I just wanted to hear your voice again."

Warmth spreads like a wildfire throughout my body.

It's two in the morning, and he's thinking about me. He was thinking about me when I was thinking about him.

"Goodnight, Finn."

I open Emily's back door and take my seat back by Ryan. The rest of the night is friendly, but it's not the same as how our Christmas movie nights were in high school. I'm with my friends, but it's like I'm watching a movie scene play out that I wasn't given the script for. It's a movie I was never meant to be in. Emily sits beside me on the sofa, and it's like I'm sitting next to a stranger. So much has happened in my life that she doesn't know about. We've barely talked in months, and I don't even know how to begin a conversation with her now. Someone who used to know every detail about my life feels like she's now worlds away. My heart hurts knowing that Finn was right. I never thought my best friend could just so easily move on without me while I was stuck missing her.

I can finally breathe a sigh of relief once I'm back in my car. I crank up the heat, turn on the Christmas music station, and sing along for the short drive home. I'm determined not to let this night ruin my Christmas. I pull into the driveway and finally get to see Dad's Christmas lights all hung up.

Inside, Dad and Lucas are making hot chocolate while Charlotte sits on the couch, scrolling on her phone.

"Charlotte," I say. "Come on, let's make some Christmas cookies."

15

On Christmas morning, I wake up to a silent house. The sun is only just beginning to rise, and I tiptoe downstairs. I open the fridge, and the light washes over the still-dark kitchen. The dough Charlotte and I mixed last night is sitting front and center, ready to go. My hands go right to work rolling the dough out and lining it with a layer of my butter, brown sugar, and cinnamon mixture. Carefully, I cut the dough into perfect rolls and place them in the oven. Soon, the aroma of my homemade cinnamon rolls fills the air as the rest of my family comes downstairs.

"The tradition lives on," Dad says.

"Absolutely." I read some baking blog about homemade cinnamon buns years ago, and ever since, it's been my tradition to make them every Christmas morning. At least this is exactly the same as it was last year. Maybe, even though I'm away for college, not everything has to change. I know for a fact we'll have cinnamon buns next year, and the next, and the next.

Dad puts on Christmas music, and we exchange gifts. When I pull the cinnamon buns out of the oven, they're perfect. The edges are brown, which is exactly how I like them. I drizzle a good helping of my homemade vanilla bean icing on top, then step back and admire my creation. I've missed this so much, being able to have the time to bake something completely from scratch.

"Breakfast is ready," I say, and everyone comes in. I mentally add five hours to the time displayed on our kitchen clock. It's already midafternoon in England.

As soon as we finish breakfast, I grab my coat and sit on our front steps to give Finn a call. There's no white Christmas this year, but the chill in the air embraces me as soon as I step outside.

"Happy Christmas," he answers. His voice makes me want to melt into my porch like a snowman who's been out in the sun too long.

"Merry Christmas. How's everything going?"

"I'm glad you called, actually," Finn says. "I'm sitting in the marina house reading because I needed to get away from that boat."

"Is it that bad?"

"No matter who you're with, it gets to be pretty annoying when you're all crammed together in a tiny houseboat. I just needed a break from it all, really."

I picture Finn curled up in some red plush armchair in a dark marina house, all alone with some classic. I bet he's wearing some thick sweater and clutching his coffee cup.

"How's your family?" he asks.

"They're good. Charlotte and I have been making a lot of cookies, and I made everyone cinnamon buns this morning." I fill Finn in on all our Christmas traditions.

"And Emily and Ryan?"

I sigh. "It's fine. I guess." I tell Finn about our Christmas party and how things feel a little different with my friends now. "I'm actually kind of happy to be going back to London."

"I never thought I'd hear those words come out of your mouth," Finn says. "Ready to come back to London."

"Shocking, right? I'm actually counting down the days until I get to go back." *The days I get to go back and see you again.*

There's silence for a moment. "I miss you," Finn finally says.

"I miss you too."

"I can't stop thinking about you. Ever since…" His voice trails off, but I fill in the rest of the sentence. *Ever since Hyde Park.* Ever since the night I couldn't stop thinking about him. "Anyway, I'm glad you'll be back in a week. And everyone else. It'll be nice to have us all back together. London was quite lonely with Queen Victoria House empty. We'll have to make the most of the semester before you leave for good."

Finn can't stop thinking about me? The words sing in

my heart. All this time, he's been thinking about me when I've been thinking about him. I'm super eager to go back to London now. At least there I have friends who actually miss me and want to see me again. There won't be anything different about returning to London and my life there will fall right back into place, like I'd hit pause for a few weeks.

———

On Christmas day, my family has this weird tradition of eating spaghetti. It's strange, but my dad always brings up the point that Christmas dinner is pretty much Thanksgiving dinner repeated and that would take away the significance of Thanksgiving. So, we've always done spaghetti instead. And even though I didn't have a Thanksgiving dinner this year, I don't protest our spaghetti tradition.

In the kitchen, Dad's hard at work mixing the tomato sauce. It's the one day out of the entire year Dad actually makes homemade tomato sauce. And since his mother is Italian, it always tastes amazing.

The fun of opening presents has worn off, but the excitement of all the new things we got puts us in a good mood. I'm itching to try out the new watercolor paint set Charlotte got me. And I'm sure Charlotte and Lucas want to try out their new gifts too. But that doesn't stop us from dragging out dinner a tad bit longer and enjoying our conversation.

We all disperse after dinner, and I fly up to my room. My easel has a fresh canvas already set up on it, and I tear the plastic wrap off my new paints. There's something about setting up my art supplies that excites me. It could be that it's the feeling of creating something, or the fact that I haven't been able to for months, or a little bit of both. I put on some soft indie music, my favorite background noise for painting, and get to work mixing the paints together to create the perfect blue-gray color.

I don't need a minute to think about what I'm going to create. As I spread my mixed color across the canvas, the cloudy sky starts to come to life. With the most careful brush strokes, the outline of Tower Bridge appears. I dip my brush in black and sharpen the outline. I add small strokes of gray to create depth. It's a long process, but it's calming. I've missed this. I consider bringing a few art supplies back with me, but it'd just be more baggage to pack up in the end and more expensive luggage fees.

I move on to the River Thames. My big brush runs back and forth on the canvas in a deep blue. I blow on the stretch of color, begging it to dry quickly. I mix my navy and white paint and get to work on highlighting and contrasting the river to make it pop. Slowly, my painting comes to life. I touch up my outlines and breathe a sigh of relief.

It's finished. And it's absolutely perfect.

I leave it up on my easel so I can admire it for the rest of break, but I can't wait to wrap it up with leftover wrapping paper and pack it in my suitcase. It'll be the perfect belated Christmas gift for Finn. A reminder of our year together in London. Something he can have to think of me once I'm back in Massachusetts.

As if on cue, my phone vibrates, and it's a message from him:

Goodnight, Livy. I'm counting down the days until we're back in the same city.

A warm, fuzzy feeling spreads through me, and I can't stop my lips from smiling. I flop down on my bed and read Finn's text over and over. I imagine him in the houseboat thinking of me and typing out that message. Then I imagine him falling asleep with me as the last thing on his mind, just like I will tonight. Once I let my mind wander, there's no stopping all the scenarios my brain creates. It's like I've opened Pandora's box. Even though the excitement from Christmas is wearing off, the same feelings are back as I count down the days until I'm back with Finn.

———

The stretch between Christmas and New Year's makes time stand still. Nothing matters during that time, and no one knows what day it is. It's the feeling of something old coming to an end and the promise of something new around the corner. It's during this time that I drive down to Duke's to see what Sandy and Marc have in their dessert case.

Duke's is a short drive, only far enough to listen to one song. Sometimes two if you're lucky and get stuck at the light. I pull into a parking spot and take a seat at the counter. In the corner, Marc's Christmas tree is still out and cluttered with homemade decorations from all the local kids. Christmas music from the jukebox fills the air because Sandy always insists that Christmas isn't over until the New Year. Sandy's busy behind the counter, filling her case with freshly baked gingerbread men.

"Olivia, honey," she says. "Wonderful to see you here again." She places a peppermint hot chocolate in front of me in my favorite pink, polka-dot mug. Duke's has a mismatched variety of funky patterned mugs Sandy's found over the years in thrift stores and while traveling. You never know what kind of mug your drink will come in.

Sandy rests her elbows on the counter across from me. "How're things? It's been too long since I've seen you at my counter."

It's funny how going to Duke's after school with Emily and Ryan used to be part of my routine. Sandy was the one who helped me decide between wearing a purple or blue prom dress my senior year. She's the reason I passed my government and economics class. *I own a restaurant with my husband*, I remember her saying when I first asked her for homework help. *Of course I understand economics.* She was the one who I truly confessed my fears to about being in London alone. *Olivia*, she'd said. *I think you'll find that you're much stronger than you think.* I didn't believe her at the time, but she was right. Somehow, Sandy was always right.

"London's actually been pretty amazing," I say. "But I think I've got a bit of a problem."

She rests her head on her hand. "Uh-huh," she says. "What's going on?"

"I have this friend in London, and we've really gotten close," I say. Memories of Hyde Park cloud my head again. "And now that I'm away from him and back home, I can't stop thinking about him. He even said he can't stop thinking about me. But I only have one semester left." I sigh. "After that, I'll be back here and going to BSU like I was supposed to. There's no way anything could ever work out between us. But I feel like something could be there, and I really don't know what to do now."

Sandy slowly nods. "I see," she says. "Love's never easy, dear. Whether or not you end up with him, it'll all be alright. Sometimes, there are some boys who are just better off as friends. Sometimes, there's more to it. And I think no matter what happens, you'll find a way to be there for each other, even if you just stay friends. You have it so easy these days with all the technology. I remember one summer when I was sixteen, we took a trip out to the beach. I met a boy named Tom, and we fell madly in love. But when it was time for my family to leave, that was it. I never saw Tom again. But with this boy, you have ways to stay in touch."

I nod. "We've been talking on the phone over break." I fill Sandy in on all our conversations.

Sandy puts her hand on my arm. "See? That's proof already. I think you'll be surprised that things just have a way of working themselves out. I was devastated I had to leave Tom. But a year later, I met Marc at a community center dance. If it had worked out with Tom, I'd never have gone to that dance by myself. And you know Marc and I were made for each other. So just have faith that everything will work out as it should."

I take another sip of my hot chocolate and let the warmth of the drink spread through my body. "Thanks, Sandy. I think I just needed to talk things out."

"Anytime," she says. "That's what I'm here for."

16

On the morning of my flight, my entire family cries when they drop me off at the airport. Even I'm in tears leaving them, knowing I won't get to see them again until May. Emily sent me a text earlier saying goodbye, and I sent a simple goodbye back. I can't bring myself to say anymore since I'm still a little hurt she moved on with her life so easily without me. If it wasn't for my scholarship program, none of this would've happened. But instead, I'm on a plane back to England.

As the plane takes off, I plug in my earbuds and put on a movie to try to make the time go by faster. Just seven hours until I get to be back in my new favorite city with Finn and hear his wonderful accent in person.

I'm jet-lagged when we land in Heathrow, but I don't care this time. The hour-long Tube journey back to Queen Victoria House stretches on for an eternity. I count down each stop. I shove my earbuds in and click through the songs on my playlist, getting bored with each one after only thirty seconds. I check my phone. No text from Finn yet, but he knows I'm on my way back.

My leg's bouncing, and a woman sitting across from me is staring at it. Two more stops. The train's doors open and close. My body sways with the train as we rush to our next stop. One more to go. My whole body's buzzing with electricity, and I jump up to my feet before the train has even stopped at the station.

I have about a mile walk from the station to Queen Victoria House. My exhaustion evaporates, replaced by pure adrenaline, as I force my legs to take each step a bit faster than the last. I'm practically sprinting once I get to the private driveway, and my suitcase bounces behind as it catches on the steps that lead to the front door.

I dig in my purse for my ID card and slam it on the key reader. It seems like ages until it flashes green. I throw open the front door and find Gabriel at the front desk, exactly where he should be.

"Hi," Gabriel says. *Oh, how I've missed chatting with him.* "Did you have a good time at home?"

I nod. "Yeah, it was fine, but it's good to be back."

"Hey, I was meaning to ask you," he says. "Over break, I got these connections with this super cool band one of my neighbors happens to know. He made it sound like he's going to be able to get me some tickets in the future for their London show. Do you, uh, think Bailey would possibly want to go with me? Since she's into music and all. I don't know. I thought maybe she'd be interested?"

"Gabriel, yes, absolutely! Bailey would be the perfect person," I say. I want to skip down the hallway because this is such exciting news. I can't wait to tell Finn. Who would've thought Gabriel would make a move on his own?

As much as I want to keep talking to Gabriel, I'm way too eager to drop off my stuff and get to the caf where I'm meeting everyone for lunch. When I unlock my door, my room's exactly how I left it—plain and boring, my bed still unmade. I unpack my suitcase and set Finn's present on my desk. I'll give it to him after lunch when it's just the two of us. I shove my suitcase back to its place in the corner, then head out to the caf.

Bailey, Hannah, and Ronan are already there at our usual table, in the middle of a deep conversation. It's like we never left.

"Olivia!" Ronan yells. "Welcome back. Did you just get in?"

I can't stop myself from smiling. I didn't realize how much I missed my friends here.

"I literally just got back and rushed over here. I'm starving. And tired," I say.

"Jet lag is the worst," Bailey says. "I got back yesterday and still feel like I'm struggling."

But with her long, blonde hair curled and her face dusted with just a hint of makeup, I'd have no idea Bailey was still adjusting to the time. I'm desperate for a shower.

I'm still wearing my leggings and sweatshirt from the plane and my hair is in a loose braid.

I go and get the caf's specialty sandwich for the day, roasted chicken with cranberry sauce, and return to our table to catch up with everyone about their break. Bailey went skiing in Utah, while Hannah and Ronan got to spend New Year's together in Manchester. They also went to Paris for the weekend. The perks of living and dating in Europe— just casually going to Paris for the weekend. No big deal.

"Where's Finn?" I ask. I figured he was running late, but it's been twenty minutes now, and he's not here. I know he's back because he told me he was returning to London on New Year's Day. The absolute earliest he could leave Liverpool. And he knew I was coming back to London today. He definitely would've seen the group text Bailey sent out about us all getting lunch today. I'd just assumed he'd come too.

"Oh, he's at Georgia's," Ronan says. "He went over to her flat this morning for something and hasn't been back since."

I hold back all the words I want to say and place my fork down. Any appetite I had vanishes as if Ronan's just performed a spell on me. Finn and I had been counting down the days until we could see each other again, and he seriously went to Georgia's on the day he knew I got back?

My stomach burns, and I force myself to eat another bite of my sandwich. I should've told him over the phone how I felt about him. How I could only think about him over break and that Ryan suddenly didn't seem like the one I was in love with. Now I'd for sure missed my chance—he was choosing Georgia. He was always going to choose Georgia.

I don't even know what my friends are talking about because I haven't been listening. I've tuned out all the noise around me. I picture Finn in Georgia's bed, where they're together under her blankets. He has his shirt off and his hands on her body as he gently kisses her. She has her hands in his hair as she messes up his curls, but he doesn't care because he's with her.

I want to scream. I wish Georgia had moved far away for university so Finn never could've reconnected with her. And I hate myself for even thinking it, but I don't care. I don't want to know Finn's with another girl.

"I'm really jet-lagged from the flight," I say, which isn't exactly a lie. "I think I'm going to head back and take it easy."

"I'll go back with you," Bailey offers.

We cross the street to make our way back to Queen Victoria House, the walk feeling like a blur all around me.

"I'm so glad you're back," Bailey says. "Apparently, Hannah and Ronan have gotten pretty serious. Hannah said Ronan drove over to see her a lot over break. I'm happy for them, but they just can't get enough of each other. It's nice having you back to balance things out. Even though I only got here one day before you, I was starting to feel a bit like a third wheel."

"You know, I'm actually really glad to be back too," I say. *Except for the whole Finn situation.* At least Bailey, Hannah, and Ronan were happy to see me.

Bailey scans her card, and we walk inside Queen Victoria House. Gabriel has a note on his desk saying he's grabbing lunch and will be back in thirty minutes, which is unfortunate because now would've been a perfect opportunity for them to talk to each other. Plus, talking to Gabriel always makes things better.

But when we walk into the lobby, I stop in my tracks. Finn's sitting right there in one of the lobby chairs with Georgia's manicured hand on his thigh. Her long, brown hair twists in perfect curls and falls down her back in an effortless ponytail. Even though she's just wearing black jeans and a sweater, she's a thousand times more put together than I ever could be. I'm now even more self-conscious about my sweatshirt and ratty braid.

Finn glances over at us, and our eyes meet. He purses his lips like he's disappointed that I walked in on them while they were sitting in the lobby on full display for everyone to see. He breaks eye contact and drops his head.

"Bailey," Georgia says. She jumps up and gives Bailey a hug. "I hope you had the best holiday. What'd you do?"

Finn says nothing to me or Bailey, not even a hello or welcome back. He sits there staring off into space while Bailey and Georgia catch up. How could he say he missed me and was counting down the days, then not even make an effort to see me?

"It was so great to see you," Georgia says. "I'm sure I'll be seeing you around."

My head spins, and my vision goes blurry. I don't even want to try to imagine Finn and Georgia spending every moment together. He's complained about her so much to me, but I guess he's still in love with her. I'm stupid for even thinking he might have thought of me in that way despite everything that's happened between us.

I might've been wrong about everything being the exact same in London. At least, it's not the same with Finn.

I go back to my room and throw Finn's present in my closet. I don't even care if it gets ruined. There's no way I'm giving it to him tonight or any time soon. I gather up my toiletries and take a nice, long shower. I fully believe warm showers can cure anything and take your mind off everything. I let the water run over me and relax my mind and body before bed.

I cut off the water and take my time with my evening skincare routine, reminding myself that I'm trying to relax. Like Sandy said, no matter the outcome, everything will work out as it should.

I'm just finishing up putting my moisturizer on when a door down the hall slams, and voices roar like a sudden clap of thunder. I shouldn't be nosy, but I can't help it. I press my ear against the bathroom door.

"You always do this," a voice shouts. A voice that sounds exactly like Finn's but loud and frustrated, the kind of tone that only comes out when a physics problem stumps him.

I can't make out what Georgia says back, but their muffled voices are tinted with anger. I've never heard Finn argue like this before. Or rather, I've never heard him argue with anyone ever. It's hard for me to even imagine what he looks like in the hall.

"Georgia," Finn yells out as if a knife has been dragged across him.

"I'm done dealing with you, Finn," she shouts, and her heels stomp down the hallway. I can picture her long ponytail swishing behind her as she leaves. I stay in the bathroom until I don't hear her footsteps anymore. It's quiet, so I open the bathroom door just wide enough to see out. No sign of Finn or Georgia.

I go back to my room and change into some sweatpants and a BSU T-shirt. I should just focus on unpacking and not worry about their business, but I can't help myself. I can't go on with my day without knowing what's going on and what might've happened over break. I go down the hall and knock on Bailey's door.

"Hey," she says. "Everything okay?" Her blonde waves are pulled up into a top knot, and she's holding a blue ceramic mug. It's not that important, but I can't turn back now.

"Yeah," I say. "Can I come in for a second?"

Bailey makes me a cup of chamomile tea, and we sit on her little white futon.

"I'm pretty sure I heard Finn and Georgia fighting. I

didn't mean to be listening, but I was coming out of the bathroom, and I could hear it in the hallway," I say. "Did you hear anything?"

Bailey takes a sip of tea. "I'm pretty sure the whole hall heard them yelling. It's so strange," she says.

"Interesting," I say. "I don't know what's going on."

"Well," Bailey says. "If he were to confide in anyone, it'd be you."

I about fall off of the futon. "Me?"

Bailey nods. "He's super close with you. He's always sitting next to you in the caf, and you guys actually hang out and study together. He never did any of that with us last year. He was either with Georgia or studying in his room alone. Sometimes, he'd hang out with Ronan, but he was always pretty quiet."

"Really?"

"He's a completely different person than he was last year when he's around you. Like, he actually seems happy." Bailey goes on to tell me about how much Finn has changed since last year. "I'm starting to think that maybe Georgia isn't the best influence on him. I don't know. He's just made some comments that make me wonder. It's so weird, because she's super friendly and easy to be around, but then hearing them yelling at each other right now? If I were him, I wouldn't keep putting up with that. I wish he would see that."

"I just want him to be happy," I say. Because no matter what happens between me and Finn, I know he deserves happiness. Especially with everything he's gone through in the past few years.

I spend some more time in Bailey's room catching up with her and seeing her ski trip pictures. Before I know it, hours have passed. It used to feel like this when Emily and I would hang out at one of our houses and just talk. We could talk about everything and anything, and time always seemed to fly. I never thought things could ever feel awkward between us. When I finally leave Bailey's room, I find myself thanking her for such a good time. I didn't realize how much I needed girl time.

"Of course," she says like it's nothing. "I'm your friend. That's what friends are for."

———

Normally, I would go to bed early, especially when I'm jet-lagged, but I can't stop myself from flipping open the sketch-book I'd brought back with me. This semester, I'm taking Introduction to Architecture, and I'm already bubbling with excitement. In preparation for the class, our professor sent out an email asking us to sketch a building we love from our hometown as an icebreaker. I debated between a few places but finally settled on an old church in Bartonsville. The small white church has been around since the 1800s, and I've always loved seeing it with the fall leaves buried around it.

I've barely scratched the surface of my drawing since I keep erasing and restarting. I need this to be perfect to make a good impression of myself and Bartonsville. I'm letting myself lose track of time and fighting against my growing tiredness when a knock at the door breaks my concentration. I have no idea who'd be looking for me this late at night.

I open the door just a crack and there he is. Finn. The boy my heart was just longing for less than twenty-four hours ago. I don't really want to see him right now, not after he completely ignored me this afternoon. I'm tempted to shut the door on him and all my silly feelings.

"Hi," Finn says before I can do anything. "When Georgia broke up with me before break, you said you were here if I needed anything. Does that offer still stand?"

I open my door all the way. How can I say no to him when I had, after all, promised that? "Of course. Come on in."

Finn reaches for my blanket as always and gets comfortable. "I'm sorry," he says. "It wasn't what it looked like in the lobby. We're not back together, in case you were wondering."

"What's going on then?" It sure looked like they were back together.

"She said she wanted to see me. I tried to tell her no since I was finally starting to move on from her and accept that our relationship was over. But she told me she had something from my mother she'd found and wanted to give it to me."

Finn pulls the blanket tighter around him and sighs.

"I should've known better. I get there, and it's literally just an old text message from my mum to her asking if she could borrow her shoes for an event. So I tried to leave so I could make it to lunch to see you, but it was like I was trapped there. She was saying how much she missed me over the holidays and how hard it must've been for me not having her. And I guess I started to believe her like I always end up doing somehow. She kept making promises that things could be better now that we'd had space. I guess I wanted to believe that would be true after being alone during the holidays."

His fingers fiddle with the corner of the blanket. "Then she offered to come back to QVH to help me clean my room. The whole Tube ride here, she just kept going on and on about how I must've been so miserable and helpless without her. By the time we got to the lobby, I sort of just snapped. I remembered what you said, that I'm not broken. I tried to tell her, but she shut me down. Then, when you and Bailey walked in, she tried to make it seem like everything was fine with us.

"But it was all building up in me, and I let it out. I told her how I'm so tired of trying to do everything up to her standards, then getting accused of not spending enough time with her when I'm hurting. I couldn't take it anymore. She just complained that I have too much baggage and that no one will ever love me like she did. It was, quite honestly, a mess. But that's how it's been lately. I mean, it's just been a pattern that's kept repeating itself since the start of this year. Every time I think I'm trying to make things better with us, it ends up so much worse."

"Finn," I say gently. "I don't think any relationship is supposed to be that much work."

"It's just stupid of me, really, isn't it?" He shakes his head. "I fall for it every single time. I thought this would fix things, and even though I know she's not good for me, I wanted her back for a moment. I thought we could talk things through, and everything could go back to how it used to be."

"It's never going to be the same, Finn. And that's okay. Letting go is hard, but you don't know what the future holds for you. There's so much to come that you don't know about. And if you're stuck mourning a failed relationship, you're going to miss out on all the good that this change can bring. When you can open your arms and embrace it, it gives you so much power. I hated that I had to come here but look what happened when I finally allowed myself to open my heart to London. I hated the change, but without it, I'd never have met you. And that's such a good thing that's come from all this."

He nods. "I guess so."

"It's what you always told me, that things would never be the same. When I went back home, things were different with my friends. You were right."

"Speaking of friends, how are things going with Ryan?" he mumbles.

"Huh?"

"Ryan," he says, still avoiding my eyes. "How's your new relationship going with the long distance?"

I take a deep breath. "It's not," I say. "We're just friends. I didn't tell him anything."

Finn finally meets my eyes. "You didn't? Why not?"

"The timing didn't feel right." *Because I could only think about you, Finn, when I looked into Ryan's eyes.* "Maybe once I'm home for good, I'll talk to him." Once I'm back in Bartonsville, things will be different. Maybe Ryan is the one because nothing could work out with Finn. Not when I only have a few more months here. And not when he's still hung up on Georgia. I was foolish to think there was ever a chance with him.

Finn nods. "Probably the better thing to do. I'm glad you're back, Livy. It truly was lonely here without you."

"It's good to have you back too," I say. "I missed you. I'll definitely miss you next year. Which, actually, that reminds me." I dig Finn's present out of my closet. "A late Christmas gift for you."

Finn cracks a smile and tears off the wrapping paper, revealing my canvas. He stares at it for a moment too long, and I worry that he doesn't like it. "Livy," he says. "Did you paint this?"

"Just for you, to remind you of Walking History and our time together. You know, like for next year when I'm gone."

"I can't wait to put it up on my wall," he says. He reaches into his coat pocket and hands me a small gold package. "It's not much, but I meant to give this to you before everything happened with Georgia."

I undo the gold wrapping to reveal a colorful tea towel with all of London's landmarks illustrated on it.

"Like I said, it's not a lot, but it reminded me of you," Finn said. "You know, all the colors in it and the fact that your room needed a little spicing up. And then, I figured you could have it as a reminder of here once you went back home." Finn takes out some tacks from his pocket and hangs the tea towel above my bed.

The little pop of color already makes a world of difference in my all-white room. And this was the perfect size decoration that I could easily pack up and take home.

"Finn, thank you so much. This means more to me than you could imagine."

"You're very welcome," he says. "And truly, thank you for the painting."

I can't help but feel a wave of peace compared to how I felt a few hours ago. Things would be okay this semester. I had my best friend here in London again, and he was happy to have me. That's all I could ask for.

17

EVEN THOUGH MY SPRING SEMESTER'S FULL OF NEW classes like Introduction to Architecture, one thing that's stayed the same is Walking History. The class lasts for the entire academic year, and there's been something nice about still starting my mornings with Mike's lectures.

Today, Mike's talking about British artists and showing us pictures of famous modern art pieces. Next to me, Joanne yawns.

"Art's so boring," she whispers to me.

This is one of my favorite lectures so far. Seeing all the paintings and learning about British artists and what influenced their style has me on the edge of my seat.

"Well, that's all for today," Mike says. "Hopefully, this will give you some idea about where you'll be going for today's clue."

Finn's quick to take Joanne's seat as everyone shuffles around to their partners.

"The clue today is easy," he says.

"You always think it's easy," I joke. Just like last semester, I haven't had to do much work when it comes to decoding Mike's clues.

"It's the Tate Modern. Mike was practically giving it away."

"The Tate Modern? I've been wanting to go there. I even asked Gabriel to go with me at the beginning of the year, but he said no."

The edges of Finn's lips curve up into the smallest smile. "Happy to be the one to go with you then."

We make our way to the museum on the Tube. The journey is relatively short, and the walk to the museum is breathtaking. Along the way, we pass St. Paul's Cathedral and cross over a pedestrian footbridge where Finn points out Shakespeare's Globe Theatre.

"Here's your museum, Livy," Finn says once we reach the entrance. "Per Mike's clue, we're supposed to take a picture of our favorite piece of art we see here. I'll leave that decision up to you."

I throw open the doors of the museum and soak in all the color around me as we wander through the hallways of modern art.

"Some of this looks like stuff I could make," Finn grumbles.

I shoot him a look. "Okay, sure, but do you ever go and make your own art?"

"Well, no."

"Then there you have it." I tell Finn all about my art

supplies at home and how much I love filling a canvas with all sorts of colors.

"Is that why you picked architecture as your major?" he asks.

I nod. "I know I could never have a career as an artist, but at least with architecture, you still get to draw in a way. It seemed like a more sensible option."

"Always playing it safe, Livy."

I let myself get lost in the museum, and Finn trails behind me, never complaining. He doesn't make a fuss when I want to stare at a painting for longer than most people or when I try to get the perfect angle for a picture. He just lets me be in my own little world.

"Look at all the colors in this one." I point to a bold painting filled with colorful squares. "Oh, and the design of this one."

Finn's fighting a smile, his head tilted ever so slightly to the side. "If only you'd have come here at the start of the year. You probably would've liked London a lot more."

"Hey," I say. I don't take my gaze off the painting in front of me. "I like London now."

We stroll through more of the museum, and I feel like I could spend all day here. I'll have to come back on my own one weekend when I have even more time. I wasn't afraid to explore on my own now. Just last weekend, I'd made the trip to Borough Market because I was craving the mushroom risotto I'd had there one afternoon with Bailey. No one else could come with me, but I didn't let that stop me. I was surprised at how much I enjoyed my solo outing. Even though I was happy to wander through the Tate with Finn, I found myself looking forward to when I could spend hours here alone. Already, I can't wait to get back to Queen Victoria House and make a list of all the museums I want to visit.

"We probably should leave in about ten minutes," Finn eventually says, breaking me from my art trance. "I've got a physics class after this. And you have your architecture class. There's nothing I can do to help get you out of missing a class this time."

I scroll back through all the pictures I took before deciding on my favorite piece, the one that has the most color. I add it to Finn and I's shared album of pictures for Walking History. Scrolling through the album is like our own personal memory box of all the places we've experienced together. I'm glad I'll always have this album to look back on once I'm home.

Finn's physics class is in a building not too far from my Intro to Architecture class, so we're able to take the Tube together to the same station. As we're riding the escalator out, Finn's phone vibrates in his pocket. He takes one glance at it, shakes his head, and shoves it back in.

"It's Georgia," he says. "Again."

"She's still calling you?" For the first week or so of classes, it seemed like Georgia was calling Finn every day. I'd thought things had fizzled out since I hadn't seen him decline a call in a while.

"Unfortunately," Finn says. "I haven't ever answered. It'll just give me false hope if I talk to her again."

Finn had kept his relationship issues with Georgia pretty quiet since their breakup. I wasn't sure if he'd discussed it with anyone else, but I wasn't about to talk about him behind his back.

"I don't know what she could possibly want from you, especially if she was the one who broke up with you."

Finn's quiet for a moment. "She wants control over me or something. Basically, she only wants me around when it's convenient for her. And at this point, she knows me too well. She knows exactly how to get me to do what she wants. I can't keep playing her game."

He tells me more about all the red flags he ignored when he was with Georgia. It gives me some hope that maybe he really is starting to see that he's better off without her.

We reach the building where my architecture class is first. Now that I'm finally doing a major-specific class, I've had even more motivation to do little sketches of buildings I see during my downtime. And, similar to Walking History, we sometimes get to go out to study London's architecture. It's been fascinating to learn about both modern and older building designs.

Finn's hands are in his pockets as he glances over at my building. "I guess I better get to physics," he says.

"You can't be late, Finley Abbott," I tease him. "I'm sure you don't roll into physics approximately ten seconds before it starts like you do for Walking History."

"I'm never late for physics," he assures me. "I make time for the things that are important to me."

I cross my arms and give him a side-eye. "Alright, sure." I readjust my tote bag on my shoulder. "I'll see you at dinner tonight?"

"Erm, I'm not sure." Finn chews at his bottom lip. "I've got a massive amount of physics and calculus I have to get done. Do you want to work on homework in my room beforehand?"

I tell Finn that works for me, and we agree on a time. We've just parted ways, and I'm opening the building door when Finn calls over his shoulder.

"See, I make time for the things that are important to me."

It takes everything in me not to skip all the way down the hallway to my architecture class.

18

THE SEMESTER CARRIES ON WITH MORE WALKING History excursions, a growing collection of my newfound love of architecture sketches, and afternoons spent studying in either my room or Finn's. One afternoon, Bailey texts me to come join her, Hannah, and Ronan for an impromptu picnic. Winter's chill is slowly fading away, and hints of spring have seemingly popped up overnight. It's not quite warm yet, but I've finally been able to put my jacket away for good. It'll be a nice day to sit outside again and not freeze.

Finn and I stop in a grocery store to buy a bag of oranges and a package of custard cream cookies.

"So it looks like we're at least contributing something to this last-minute picnic," Finn says.

We take the tube to Chalk Farm, and I follow him through the residential area. I've never been to Primrose Hill before. Finn told me on the Tube I'd been missing out and that it was an absolute pity I'd lived in London for a whole semester and never gone.

Primrose Hill is like any other park I've been to—green, filled with trees, and lined with paths. But as Finn and I continue on the uphill path, I understand why I've been missing out. We're on top of a mountain-sized hill and I'm above the city all over again. And it absolutely takes my breath away. Ronan waves us over to the blanket they've set up nestled on the hill's lush grass.

"Finn! Olivia!" he says. "So glad you could make it."

"Here," Finn says, tossing our cookies and fruit in the middle of the blanket. "Our small contribution."

Hannah creates a spread of cheese, grapes, and a baguette. She's even brought a bottle of red wine. It's the fanciest picnic produced by college kids I've ever seen. It's like I'm living out a movie scene.

Bailey connects her phone to a Bluetooth speaker, then flicks through her playlists before settling on some soft alternative. It's probably some small English band I've never heard of. But whoever they are, the gentle piano and guitar make for the perfect background music.

Finn sits beside me and cuts a piece of baguette. He taps me on the shoulder and nods his head toward the blanket to our right. A girl is lying on top of her boyfriend, and they're kissing like they haven't seen each other in a hundred years. The boyfriend rubs his hands over her back, and I look away out of fear that he's going to take her shirt off.

"Ew," I say.

Finn raises his eyebrow. "Ew?"

"Yes, ew. Why are they doing that in the park where everyone can see?"

"Public display of affection. Emphasis on the public part." Finn glances over at the couple again. "Even heavier emphasis on the affection part."

"Yeah, they can't seem to get enough."

"That's kind of what love is," Finn says.

Double ew. I don't need that image of him and Georgia. Even if they're broken up. That could've been them at one point. Actually, it probably *was* him at some point. He must read my face because a laugh explodes out of him.

"Stop!" I smack his shoulder.

"Ow," Finn says, rubbing his shoulder in mock pain.

"Quit laughing at me." But now, I can't help but laugh at him.

"Cut it out, you two," Ronan says. He leans over and kisses Hannah.

Finn's head whips around, and he makes eye contact with me. "Ew," we say at the same time, then erupt into laughter all over again.

"I'm glad you guys could come last minute," Bailey says.

"Why hasn't Georgia been around?" Hannah asks. "She would've come to something like this last year. Did you break up again or something?"

"Hannah," Ronan warns.

Finn's face flushes red. "Erm, yeah, she did, actually,"

he says. "Right before Christmas. I haven't really wanted to talk about it." His voice trails off, and he doesn't give any more details.

"In other news," Bailey says, saving Finn from any more questions about Georgia. "Gabriel stopped me after class today and offered me tickets to this band's performance in Camden. Thoughts? It's kind of random, but I did listen to some of their music online, and it's honestly not bad. Not what I expected, but better."

Finn stifles a laugh, and I lightly punch him. "Yes, absolutely, yes. You have to go."

"I mean, I guess there's no harm in going," Bailey says.

"But it's Gabriel," Hannah points out.

"I mean, yeah. But this band is exactly the kind of music I like, and it's a free ticket. Plus, Gabriel's always been nice to me. He's super kind to Olivia."

Ronan breaks off a grape. "Maybe Olivia should go with him then."

Finn immediately interjects. "I don't see them as a good fit." I can't help but shoot him a smile. Finally, he takes my side.

"Just go," I say. "I think you'll enjoy it. He was telling me a little about the band, and it sounds like it should be a good concert."

Ronan, Bailey, and Hannah launch into a conversation about previous concerts they'd gone to in London and how cool the concert venue is. I've never heard of it, but when Gabriel was describing the place, it sounded pretty awesome.

"Hey," Finn whispers, nudging my shoulder. "Did you know there's a camel at the bottom of this hill?"

"Yeah, right," I say. "Nice one."

Finn's eyes go wide. "Do you not believe me? The boy who grew up in London? That hurts, Livy." He puts his hand over his heart.

I flick a grape at his forehead. "You're not funny."

He plucks the grape off the ground and pops it in his mouth. "It's in Regent's Park, down at the bottom of Primrose Hill. I'm serious." Finn stands up and pulls his sweater over his head. "I'll race you to the bottom and show you the camel."

"You're on," I say.

"We'll be back," Finn shouts over his shoulder to the others as he takes off down the hill. He's like a kid as he bounces down and flails his arms. I'm taking things a bit slower. The steep hill stretches out, and my legs fight not to fly out from under me. I've never been fast at races, and I have no doubt Finn's going to rub his victory in my face.

He's almost to the bottom of the hill when he trips on his own feet. He rolls down the rest of the way, and now it's my turn to laugh at him. I run down the remainder of the way to where Finn lies unmoving at the foot of the hill.

"Stop it," Finn says. He tries to hold in his laughter, but he can't. He stands up and brushes the dirt off.

"You fell down the hill," I say in between bursts of laughter.

"Piss off," he says. I can't even take him seriously.

"You've got dirt on your butt."

"Of course I do." He brushes his hands on his pants. "Let's go find this bloody camel."

We walk through the park along a dirt path under the trees as if a camel's going to suddenly appear. I'm sure he's just joking around, but I'm glad I get to have time with just him. He could've done this on purpose to—no, I'm not going to let myself think what I actually want to think.

"There it is," Finn shouts, pointing into the bushes.

"Oh, of course. There it is."

Finn shoves me closer to the bushes. "Look past them. Beyond the wire fences and you'll see the camel."

I don't believe it; Finn's right. A camel is standing there, and a second one is lying down. "What in the world?"

"It's the London Zoo," Finn says. "It backs up to Regent's Park, so sometimes, if you're lucky, you can see a few of the animals. It's the easiest way to see bits of the zoo for free."

"I can't believe this."

The corners of Finn's mouth tip upward, the smallest smile of pride filling his face. "My mum and I used to come here after I got out of school. My dad would take my sister to the flower gardens, and my mum and I would walk the park and go to the science museum."

I try to imagine Finn as a child wandering through this park. Why is it such a hard image for me to see?

"It's been really hard," he continues. "Especially with the holidays and the tension still with my dad and sister. It's going to be three years soon, but still." He sighs. "I can't believe it'll already be three years in a few weeks."

————

Deep inside the depths of the park, time seems to stop. The path we've been walking along leads us to a bridge over a canal. I rest my hands on the stone. Two kayakers paddle down in matching yellow kayaks.

"Do you think the others will wonder what happened to us?" I ask.

Finn joins me in looking out at the water. "I don't care," he says.

"But won't they care?"

"I think they'll be fine," Finn says. "They've probably gone back to Queen Victoria House by now."

Was it that late already? I check the time on my phone and see that I have a text from Bailey:

Have fun with Finn!

We walk along a canal, and I'm reminded of the night before Christmas break again. Just like London's magic in the winter, there seems to be something special in the spring air. And even though I'm still wearing a sweater in early spring, I can feel it. With all the greenery around me, it's as if London's born again. Like London, I can start all over in the spring.

Just as quickly as the leaves grew back and the flowers bloomed, the feeling washes over me.

"I'm happy," I say. Maybe it is just the change in the season, but this feeling floods my body. I want to run through the park and cartwheel across the lush grass. "I'm really, really happy here."

"I think I'm beginning to feel happier too," Finn says. "London's starting to feel more like home again, and I'm glad the city's having that effect on you as well."

"It's going to be so hard to leave at the end of the semester," I say, picturing the day that looms in the distance. The day I leave London for good. "I'm going to have to start all over at a new school and learn a new city."

I'd been to Boston a few times on school trips or with my family, but I didn't know the city like I knew London. Like it was the back of my hand.

"Well," Finn says. "You can have a home in multiple places. London will always be a home to you."

"Kind of like how London and Liverpool are home to you?"

"Liverpool's not home," he says. "It never will be."

"But your dad?" He's said before that they don't get along the best, but…

"Are you going to call him on your mom's anniversary?"

Finn's eyes drill into mine. The answer's no, for sure. It was a stupid question to ask because his mind hadn't changed overnight.

"Why would I?" he grumbles.

"Because, Finn. He's your dad. Your mom's husband. She wouldn't want to know you don't get along."

"You don't know my mum or my dad," Finn says. He picks up a rock and tosses it into the canal. "They both hated each other anyway. I can hardly remember a time when they weren't fighting."

"But he still loved her at one point, didn't he?" I say. "You even said he stayed with her up until she died."

"I never said it was the best choice," Finn exclaims. "She would've been better off without him."

"But…"

"It's a hard topic, Livy. I'd rather not talk about them now and just enjoy London as I have it."

"But you can't forget the good memories you have here."

"Sure," he says with a hint of annoyance.

He's not going to listen to anything else I have to say. I guess he has a point too. I don't know everything. It's not like I ever talked to my mom. I don't even know when her birthday is.

Birds sing a variety of melodies around us as our feet shuffle along the dirt paths. We climb back up Primrose Hill, a challenge for my now tired legs. We reach the top and see Finn is right; Hannah, Bailey, and Ronan have packed up and left. Gray clouds blanket the city's skyline, bringing the promise of an afternoon shower.

As if by some unspoken language, we sit in our original spot on the hill for one final goodbye glance at the city. My hands sink into the long strands of grass. A rush of wind tosses the tree branches around us and plays with my hair.

I'm glad that, even in the chaos of moving to London, I found Finn. I'm lucky to have him as a friend who understands how I feel.

But I can't take it anymore.

"Finn," I say.

"Yes?" His eyes meet mine, and I could melt into a puddle on the hill. His beautiful hazel eyes. I'm a goner at this point, and there's no going back. I take a deep breath. If I don't say anything now, I'm only going to keep thinking about him, and it'll end up eating me alive. It's better to know now what he's thinking too.

"What happened between us on the night before I went home for Christmas break?"

Finn breaks our gaze. He runs his fingers along the grass, and my heartbeat is loud in the silence that lingers between us.

"If you don't want to…" I say, trying to prevent myself from hearing a truth I don't want to accept. If he wanted to talk about it, he would've mentioned it. But he hasn't, and I hate that I even asked him. Of course nothing happened because we're just friends. His mind was probably still on wanting to fix things with Georgia at the time.

"Livy." Finn shakes his head. "That was the best night of my life." He breaks out into a smile. "I don't regret a single moment at all."

I'm almost positive my heart skips a beat.

"What?" After hearing what I've wanted to hear all along, that's all I manage to say?

"You're beautiful, Livy, and so fun to be around. You're part of the reason why being in London has gotten easier," Finn says. "So no, I don't have a single regret from that night."

Hold on. I don't even know where to begin to process everything he's just said. He thinks I'm beautiful? I make things better when we're together? Everything that happened that night was one hundred percent intentional. My heart beats so fast it's about to explode out of my chest, and I could do a million cartwheels down Primrose Hill. I never want this semester to end.

"I'm sorry if I overstayed my welcome that night. I should've just gone back to my room, but I was thinking about my mum and didn't want to be alone. With you, I was happy. I'm sorry if I made things uncomfortable for you," he says.

"I'm not sorry," I say. I wish we could redo that night all over again, but for real this time. I wanted Finn and me under the same duvet, sharing stories and kisses until we both fell asleep hand in hand. I'd wake up early, and he'd be annoyed but fall back to sleep while I got ready. I'd get to stare at beautiful, shirtless Finn in my bed.

"But Livy," Finn says. "I'm not sure if I'm completely over Georgia. I've been trying to let go, but we were together for so long, and I don't know if I'm ready to move on yet." He stares at the grass and adjusts his glasses. "I'm sorry. But I don't want to lose you as my best friend. I've never been happier around anyone else."

I nod. At least he's being honest with me. But the fact that I'm the one who makes him happy makes my heart skip a beat. We have plenty of time left together, but I also know the next few months I have here will fly by. Maybe this is all a phase, and once I'm back home, my feelings for Ryan will return. Or maybe I'll meet someone new. There'll be countless people at Boston Southeast to meet. Anything could happen.

"We better go back," Finn says, interrupting my thoughts. "It's nearly dinnertime, and I'm sure the others will be expecting us and wanting to know what we got up to."

"We'll just tell them we were looking for the camel," I say.

19

THE WEEKS BLEND TOGETHER AGAIN, JUST LIKE THEY DID in the fall. It's a Sunday night, and Finn and I are sitting in my room working on homework we've been procrastinating on all weekend. Or rather, I procrastinated. I ignored all my responsibilities to explore some of London's art museums by myself. Finn, at least, was studious as always, but he's keeping me company with his physics textbook.

I'm reading an article for my ethics class, but nothing's clicking in my head. I yawn and set the article aside. Finn's still lying on his stomach on my bed, his hand going a mile a minute across his notebook.

"Finn?" I ask. "Can we take a break?"

He glances up from his textbook. "A break?"

"Yeah," I say. "You've been doing physics since dinner, and this article is making me bored out of my mind."

He writes out another problem and goes at it, working to solve it.

"Finn," I say and plop down next to him on my bed. "Let's go get ice cream or something."

"It's not exactly warm outside, Livy," Finn says as he flips the page in his notebook. London has been teasing us with tastes of spring, but the evenings still have a chill in the air.

"Your point?" I tug on Finn's arm, feeling his bicep through his shirt. A tingle runs through me, and I squash my feelings right away. "Come on. I'm losing motivation. You haven't stopped doing physics all day. I think a sweet treat would help both of us."

Finn sighs and sets his pen down. He runs his fingers through his curls and meets my eyes. And when he looks at me like that, time seems to come to a standstill. He glances back at his physics textbook. It's calling his name, but he slams it shut and shakes his head.

"I just can't say no to you," he murmurs, which somehow feels strangely intimate. And before I can stop it, that tingle in my spine's back, and it's too late to do anything about it. It spreads from my arms all the way to my fingertips.

Finn shoves his textbook into his backpack, and even that motion sends a fresh wave of heat through my body. "Fine, Livy, we'll take a break," he says. "But after, I'm holing up in my room to finish physics."

"Deal," I say. I jump up and grab my coat, a great distraction from sitting next to him. I busy myself with my zipper in an effort to calm myself down. *He's just my friend*, I remind myself. And even though I take a deep breath, I can still feel bits of the tingle lingering in my toes as I follow Finn out into the hall. Thank god he's going back to his room to study after ice cream because I don't think I could handle us being together in my room right now.

———

In the morning, Finn doesn't join us for breakfast. I don't think much of it because some days he sleeps too late and just shows up to class with a cup of coffee and a grouchy mood. But when Mike starts the lecture about our next site, I'm concerned. If Finn's running late, he usually walks in right as class is starting. But as the minutes tick by, I become filled with dread.

Last night, after we got back from ice cream, he went back to his room to keep studying. He didn't seem sick or anything. Maybe he stayed up too late and forgot to set an alarm.

"Right, so now we'll all head over to Hampstead," Mike says, interrupting my train of thought.

I follow my class to the Tube station to head to Hampstead. I have no idea what we're looking for here since I wasn't paying attention. I pull my phone out and send Finn a quick text:

> Is everything alright? We're heading to Hampstead for Walking History.

When we arrive, everyone disperses with their partners to look for whatever Mike had lectured about. Bailey and I have been here before, so at least I feel comfortable walking around a familiar area by myself. I'll just explore until Finn gets here.

"Where's Finn?" Joanne asks me.

"I'm not sure."

"You can walk around with us," Alyssa offers.

"I'm fine, really. I'm sure he's on his way," I say. But when I glance at my phone, there's no reply from Finn.

Joanne and Alyssa go off on their own, and I dial Finn's number. It rings for what feels like forever until he finally answers.

"Hello?" he mumbles, his voice clouded with sleep. It's a good thing I'm waking him up if he overslept.

"Finn?" I say. "Is everything okay? You missed Walking History."

"Livy," he says. "I'm so sorry. I had a hard night last night." He pauses before adding, "I'm with Georgia."

And it feels like he wants to step on my heart and shatter it into a million pieces.

"Finn!"

"I'm really, really sorry," he practically whispers.

"We were together last night doing homework," I say gently. "I thought everything seemed fine, but if it wasn't, why didn't you tell me? I thought we could talk about the real things. I thought we were best friends."

"Olivia," Finn says. "It was a hard night. She called me, and I needed to talk to someone who'd understand, so I answered." There's a pause before he says, "I really needed her."

"But I was right there, only two doors down. It's not like you were alone, Finn. You had me. You had all of us here who would've supported you. I thought you were trying to move on from her."

"Olivia," Finn says again. "It wouldn't be the same. I had to be with her, just for the night. There's nothing you could've done. I had to be with her."

"But, Finn," my voice shakes. *There's nothing you could've done.* "I'm always here for you. Did I do something?"

"You wouldn't understand," Finn says, his voice laced with pain now. "Please, just respect that I want to be with her right now, alright? It wouldn't be the same if I were with you."

The truth has always been in the back of my mind, but I've been trying to deny that I'm just his best friend since Christmas break. Sure, he doesn't regret a thing we did before break, but Georgia still has control over his heart.

But he called me beautiful and fun to be around and said he's happiest when he's around me. I guess he only wanted to be around me when things weren't working out with her. He only wanted to spend time with me that night at Hyde Park so he wouldn't have to be alone with his thoughts. And last night, I must've been misreading everything.

He'd told me she knew how to control him. Whatever she'd said must have worked, and there must've been a reason he finally caved and answered her call.

I'm fired up now, and my feelings are hurt. I'd opened up to him; I thought he was doing the same with me. I thought we trusted each other. I've been there for him on plenty of hard nights. I've listened to him complain about Georgia. And now he just goes back to her because I'm not good enough?

"You can't keep running back to her thinking everything's going to be the same. I mean, honestly, you're kind of being a hypocrite, going on and on about how people change and nothing stays the same. Yet you still go back to your, what would you say, *bloody* ex-girlfriend, who you can't seem to get over. You love her, and you use me whenever you can't be with her," I say. "How respectable, Finley Abbott."

"Olivia," Finn's voice sounds like it could jump through my phone and strangle me. "It's the goddamn anniversary of my mother's death, okay? Can't you have a bit of respect?"

"Finn, I'm…"

"I don't think you understand how lonely and upset I've felt. I tried to hold it together last night, but I needed to be around the one person who I still talk to here who knew my mum."

"Finn, I didn't know," I say. "How was I supposed to know? Why wouldn't you tell me?"

"Just forget it, alright?" he says. "Georgia's always said that it's better to just take a day to let the pain exist. She's the only one who knows how to take care of me when I'm hurting, and she's always said I shouldn't put that burden on anyone else."

"Finn, I'm so sorry about your mom and for getting upset. But still…you could've talked to me. I thought we could talk about anything."

"You're making this all about yourself. Just like you always do. You don't know what I'm feeling," Finn grumbles. "Only Georgia understands since she's been there for me during this time for the past three years."

I don't even want to take the time to argue with him about every accusation he's made. It won't do any good. So I dig at something that I know will strike a nerve.

"Making everything about me? Says the one who I know for a fact won't even call his dad today. Talk about selfish."

"Piss off, Olivia," Finn says. Only this time, it isn't the joking *piss off*. He means it for real. There's silence, then the call ends.

There's no way I can do the sites for today, especially without my partner here. I take a deep breath, compose myself, and go into a nearby bakery. The smell of freshly baked bread greets me, and I browse the assorted baked goods sitting out on wooden trays behind the case. I'm not even hungry, but I buy a chocolate croissant anyway. There's a park close by that Bailey took me to one weekend, Hampstead Heath. Without even thinking, my feet take me there. I sit right in the grass, letting the morning dew absorb into my jeans. I don't even care that I don't have a blanket or anything to sit on.

I've ruined everything with my best friend in London. Only a few days ago, I was thinking about how sad I'd be to leave this place and now all I wanted to do was get on the next flight out. He'll never get over Georgia. It seems like no matter what happens between them, he always finds his way back to her. And even though he's my best friend here, I wonder if Georgia will always hold a higher place in his heart than anyone else.

———

Finn comes to class the next day about thirty seconds before it starts and makes a beeline to his seat with his head down. Mike offers him a sympathetic smile. Why couldn't Finn have told me it was the anniversary?

The whole class seems to drag on. My mind's still spinning, and I can't seem to focus on Mike's lecture at all. Finn already has his stuff packed up and makes a run for the door as soon as Mike dismisses us. He's so quick to leave I don't even see him up ahead of me on the street. Not that I'd want to walk back with him anyway. I knew I was making a mistake in letting myself have feelings for him. It was stupid. I'd be leaving soon, and none of this would ever matter. I'd never see Finn again or anyone else here.

I scan my Oyster card and enter the Tube station. I never really belonged here. I wish I could exit the station and appear in Boston like some magical time traveler. Life would be better in Boston. Except, Emily and I don't talk much anymore because she has Maddie. And Ryan, well, I didn't want to go home and potentially ruin another friendship because of a stupid crush.

What if I don't belong in Boston? And now, London feels foreign again. If London isn't where I'm meant to be and neither is Boston, where am I supposed to go? Just hover midair in an airplane until life works itself out?

I should've known better after reading my acceptance letter to London City University. I should've declined the offer and enrolled in some community college in Boston and transferred over after freshman year. That way, I could've still been in Boston with Ryan and Emily and spent every single weekend with them. But with the scholarship, I don't know if that would've even been an option.

Finn's words about change echo in my mind. Of course people change. Even if I did get to go to a community college, it wouldn't have been the same. Emily and Ryan might have still forgotten about me and decided I was less important once they met the all-wonderful Maddie.

I'm doing it again. Finn was right. I'm making this all about me. I'm jealous of what I can't have and only focusing on what I want at the moment.

Finn. Now I've gone and ruined things with him, my best friend here. I thought we were getting so close and now he feels like he's an entire ocean away.

I just have to survive this semester, then I can figure

out things from there. If I actually want to go to BSU or stay here. If I want to try to fix my friendship with Emily and Ryan or accept things for how they are.

20

WALKING HISTORY IS NOW MY LEAST FAVORITE CLASS. Finn has been avoiding me all week, and we haven't spoken a word. I tried saying hi to him in passing, but he tucks his head down and pretends he doesn't hear me. He still sits with our table for meals but contributes nothing to the conversation. He's either reading or doing more physics. Yesterday, he showed up with headphones on. He might as well not even sit with us if he's going to be like that.

I get up from breakfast and place my plate in the dish return area. It's time to head to class alone since Finn left early to go to the toilet so he wouldn't have to walk with me to class. Again.

"Hey," Ronan's voice catches me off guard. He doesn't have a class at this time, so he usually hangs out at breakfast a little longer than Finn and I. Ronan follows me out of the caf.

"What's been up with you and Finn?" he asks.

I shrug. "We kind of had a fight about some personal stuff, and now he hasn't talked to me since."

Ronan zips up his jacket. "Have you tried talking to him?"

"I don't think he wants anything to do with me right now."

"Listen, Olivia," Ronan says. "Whatever happened, it doesn't make any sense. You and Finn were practically inseparable."

My heart sinks when I'm reminded of all my happy memories with Finn. We *were* inseparable. And now it feels like we're strangers. My feelings are hurt and the only person I want to talk to is the one person who I can't. Finn would know what to say. Finn would listen to me. But I don't have him anymore.

"I miss him," I admit to Ronan. "But honestly, I don't think he wants to talk to me. Every time I try to say something, he ignores me. He makes excuses for why he can't be around me. At this point, I don't really know what to do."

"I just find it odd," Ronan says. "Especially considering what he said to me one time."

I can't stop my curiosity from spilling out. "What did he say?"

"It was just a passing comment," Ronan says. "But he made it seem like he was a lot happier with you than he was with Georgia."

If Ronan had told me those words a month ago, I

would've fainted on the spot. But now, it doesn't matter. If there was ever a chance he might've had feelings for me at one time, it's gone now. Especially if he keeps running back to Georgia. And especially after our sort of fight.

"Well, there's zero chance of him ever admitting that now. Pretty sure all feelings he might've had are gone."

Part of me wishes Ronan hadn't told me because now my mind can't stop going down the *what if* paths the entire Tube ride to class. What if I said something to him before I went home for Christmas break? What if I acted more romantic toward him at Hyde Park? What if I'd admitted my feelings after my plane landed in Boston? What if we never had a fight, and Finn could be kissing me now instead of ignoring me? What if what Ronan was saying was true?

What if I've been wrong about everything all along?

———

Finn, of course, doesn't acknowledge me in class. He arrives at class approximately ten seconds before it starts, and when Mike dismisses us, he bolts out of his chair. There's no time for me to try to say anything to him unless I were to go knock on his door. Which I'm not going to do either. What if Georgia's in there? What if he's not there and is at Georgia's? I don't even know if they're back together, but there's still a chance he could be with her.

My dorm room feels a thousand times lonelier than

it's ever felt. I'm thankful Ronan and I even had a semi-conversation this morning, but it's not like I can consider him as a close friend. And Bailey and Hannah hadn't invited me to do anything recently. Hannah and Ronan were always with each other, and now that Bailey and Gabriel were starting to hang out after their concert outing, they were spending every free minute together browsing through their record collections.

My own friends in Massachusetts could hardly be considered my friends now. I actually tried to call Emily last week, but she was too busy with her own life to talk. I should call Ryan, but I bet he's busy doing whatever and becoming better friends with Emily and Maddie.

I wish things would go back to how they were. I wish Finn was sitting in my room, even if he's ignoring me to work on physics. I want him here. I miss having him, even if I only get to have him as a friend. But I don't know how anything's going to change between us.

Everything I'd been looking forward to about going back to Massachusetts had let me down and now the same thing had happened when I returned to London. I put my faith too much in people only to be disappointed.

I don't know what I want. I don't know what city or place is going to make me happy or if I'm going to be disappointed in every place I go. This time, a face mask or a hot shower aren't going to solve my problems. I'm not even going to try. I don't bother going to dinner that night. I throw on my llama pajama pants, turn out the lights, bury my head in my pillow, and cry.

I DON'T INTEND TO WAKE UP AS EARLY AS I DO ON A Saturday, but I'm wide awake at five in the morning. Like, full-on wide awake. There's no chance I'll be able to fall back asleep, so I spend extra time on my morning routine. I have enough time to do a full yoga practice, then take advantage of the open water closets and get a long, warm shower. The caf opens later on the weekends, so I eat a protein bar and some yogurt in my room. I even spend extra time drying my hair and putting on makeup, but it's still only seven when I'm done.

I doubt many other students would be awake and ready to go on with their day this early on a Saturday. I can either sit in my room until someone wakes up for breakfast, or I can take control of my choices for once. I lace up my shoes and walk out of my room. A little way down the road is a park and pond I've been meaning to explore but haven't gotten around to.

A few elderly couples stroll down the paths together. I take a seat on a wooden bench and watch the swans glide in the small pond. In the distance, I can make out London's skyline. It's quiet, and a wave of peace rushes over me. Right now, I'm alone, one with me and my thoughts.

A runner with floppy, black curls dashes down the path. One other younger person who's awake early. As the runner gets closer, I recognize those black curls as Ronan's.

"Fancy seeing you here," he says. He stops to catch his breath and sits beside me.

"Hey, Ronan," I say. "I didn't know you were an early riser."

"Eh, only sometimes on the weekends when I feel like exercising early. Today was one of those days." He chugs some of his water. "Hey, have you talked to Finn yet?"

I sigh. "It's pointless." For some reason, I trust Ronan a little more. Or I'm desperate to talk to someone at this point. So I spill all the details to Ronan. "He's been avoiding me, and I don't even know how I feel anymore. About him, about London, about life," I conclude.

"Olivia," Ronan says. He puts his sweaty hand on my shoulder. "Listen, you've got to talk to him."

I push away his hand. "Too sweaty, I just showered."

"You need to talk to him," Ronan repeats.

"Why in the world would I do that? He doesn't want to talk to me. He doesn't even want to look at me."

"Finn's not going to be the one to say anything first. I know that about him," Ronan says. Maybe Ronan's right. Finn did make comments about his dad and how they've been on bad terms since his mom died. Finn's never tried to fix things with him or tell him how he's feeling. And that's his own family member.

"He'll keep the tensions going forever," Ronan continues. "But I know he fancies you."

"But—"

"He's not going to make a move or say how he feels. You're only here for a short amount of time, and listen, Olivia, he once told me that he's lost so much in his life that now he's afraid of losing you."

"What?"

"I could tell by the way he looks at you and from everything you two would do together that he might have some feelings for you. But I think he was worried about there being some guy back at home you liked? And knowing you wouldn't be here for very long was probably another thing holding him back."

It all starts to make sense. "Oh my god."

"And even though he seems rightly miserable with Georgia these days, I think he's just going to keep running back to her because he's afraid to fully let her go," Ronan says. "That's why I keep telling you to talk to him. Otherwise, it's just going to be an endless cycle for him. Nothing's going to change with your current situation. Just think about it."

"I will," I say.

"Good." Ronan jumps up from the bench and jogs off. "Catch you later," he yells over his shoulder.

I take a deep breath. I always have a choice in how events play out. I can either try to fix things or let things stay as they are. I don't want to leave England with this tension between us. I want to at least know I tried the best I could to fix things with Finn. I want to know I at least had a chance at loving him.

Ronan's words finally sink in. All this time, Finn's been just as afraid of change as me. So afraid of change and losing a piece of his mother forever that he's willing to cling to Georgia, the person he'd had here when his mom was still alive. I can't blame him. All this time he'd done so much to help me adjust to London while still struggling to grasp all the changes he'd gone through. Of course he'd be afraid to let go of the last thread of the familiar. He was clinging to home just like I'd tried to.

Then there's Emily and Ryan. It does feel like they've moved on, but they've been experiencing big changes too. I'm not there with them all the time like in high school, so of course they're doing things without me and spending time together and moving on with their lives. But they're happy, and they're not trying to make me feel bad. If I were there in Boston with them, they'd include me. If I return to Boston next year, it'd be weird at first, but things would eventually fall back into place. At the end of the day, they're still my friends.

That is, if I accept my admission to BSU for my sophomore year. I'd have to go through the whole change and adjustment and learn a new school and culture all over again. And I would miss getting a cider at the pubs, the views from Primrose Hill, the magic of London during Christmas, and all the friends I'd made here. I have a choice in how next year turns out. This whole time in London, I've wanted to leave and go back to the familiar when I wasn't embracing the change. I could have both. I could stay here in London and still have my summers in Massachusetts. I didn't have to delete one part of my life. I could have both if I made it happen. If I kept up communication with friends here and at home, things could be alright in both places. I could have a home in London and Bartonsville. Home didn't have to be one place or another.

All this time, I've been resisting the idea that London could be a *forever* instead of a *temporary*. Change isn't always a bad thing, and it can actually turn out for the better, even if it doesn't feel like it at the moment. With this unexpected change, I got to live in a new country, learn about the world, and meet new people. Did I really want to throw that all away when there was so much more to discover?

Maybe Ronan's right. Maybe I should take a chance and try talking to Finn.

I'm on my feet before my brain has fully decided my course of action. At this point, what did I have to lose?

I'm speed-walking through the park as if I'm racing against time to make it back to Queen Victoria House. There's no turning back now. I'm determined to talk to Finn no matter what, to do whatever I can to make things right between us.

22

I'M PRACTICALLY OUT OF BREATH WHEN I MAKE IT TO Finn's door. I bang on his door over and over, feeling like I'm going to punch a hole through it. I know I'm being dramatic, but I also know I absolutely need to talk to him now while I'm feeling confident.

After what feels like an eternity, the door finally creaks open. Finn's curls are a mess, twisting in all the wrong directions. His glasses sit lopsided on the end of his nose, and he's standing there in a black bathrobe and underwear.

I'm afraid he's going to close the door when he sees it's me. He hesitates, but he finally opens the door a little wider.

"Olivia," Finn says. He takes his glasses off and rubs his eyes. "It's eight in the morning. On a Saturday."

Oh, right. Finn never wakes up early. "Did I wake you?"

He blinks. "I'm awake now."

"I need to talk to you. Right now."

Finn sighs again and messes up his curls, but he doesn't protest. "You can come in, I guess."

He opens the door wider for me to come in. He turns on the lamp on his desk, then ties the strings of his robe around him. As he pulls back his blackout curtains, natural light floods in and illuminates the mess of his room. Piles of notebooks, open textbooks, and scrap pieces of paper crowd his desk. Two empty plastic water bottles are on the ground, along with a half-empty bottle of whiskey. A pair of dirty underwear sits in the corner by his closet. Gross, Finn.

"Erm, sorry about the state of the place," Finn says. He fixes the black duvet on his bed, then motions for me to have a seat. After placing the whiskey on his desk and putting the underwear in his hamper, he joins me on his bed. He yawns and rubs his eyes again.

I don't want to waste another minute, so I dive headfirst into everything. "Finn, I'm sorry for how I acted toward you and for being self-centered. I'm sorry for not caring as much as I should've. I'm sorry for whatever I said and did that hurt you. I miss the friendship we used to have."

Finn doesn't say anything, so I keep talking to fill the silence. "I don't want to keep on going with this weird tension. You're my best friend here. I don't want to lose that."

"It's my fault," Finn finally says. "You didn't know it

was her anniversary." He swallows and fiddles with his robe string. "I'm the worst at admitting when I'm wrong. And I have an even harder time saying I'm sorry. But I'm genuinely sorry for the way I've treated you these past few weeks. It wasn't fair of me. I can't blame you for not knowing how I was feeling because I hadn't told you everything. I'm not really the best at talking about my feelings."

"I thought we could be open with each other," I say. "I've told you about everything I've been struggling with this year."

Finn shakes his head. "It's not so easy for me. No one here knows about my mum. Well, no one except you. There are times when I'm feeling so low and empty when I'm really missing her, and it feels like there's no one here who could possibly understand me."

"Is that why it seems like you're avoiding us sometimes?"

"Physics homework," Finn says, finally meeting my eyes. "It's the only way I can get my brain to not think about her. If I just keep my mind focused on physics, I can distract myself from anything else I'm feeling. It's my only outlet."

All those days at dinner when Finn was studying or working on problems weren't because he wanted to get his work done. He must've been hurting all those times and was trying his best to keep himself together. My heart sinks. We shouldn't have been teasing him about his study habits. But we had no way of knowing.

Finn yawns again. "It's still extremely hard when this time of year comes around. I don't, erm, I guess I still don't really know how to handle things."

Of course he didn't. No nineteen-year-old should be suffering the way he is. "I know you mentioned that you don't get along with your dad, but I feel like he's one of the only people who would really understand how you're feeling. Or your sister, even."

"Olivia," Finn says. "I love that you have the relationship you have with your family, but mine's not like that. It was like this even when my mum was still here." He catches himself for a moment. "They'd been arguing constantly since I was twelve. I still hate my dad for breaking her heart, even if he chose to stick around with her until the end. And now, like on Christmas, my dad doesn't seem to understand that you can still be sad three years later. My sister just gets on to me about being moody and ruining our family time together. It's like I'm the only one who still notices that she's gone."

"I wouldn't say that."

"Yes, well," he says. "You haven't met my family. Anyway, I'm truly sorry for how this year's ending. But I need you to understand why I've been at Georgia's place. She knew my family extremely well. She knew my mum. So when I'm with Georgia, I feel like I'm allowed to be sad. And Georgia can remind me of memories about my mum that I've forgotten. It's like a way of still holding on to her."

"I understand," I say, because I do. I get it. I know

he's still clinging to what he doesn't have anymore. "I think you're afraid of change."

Finn takes off his glasses and rubs his eyes. He doesn't say anything for a while. He sets his glasses back on and lets out a breath. "I guess it started to occur to me that I was trying so hard to make a failing relationship work. Even though we were broken up, I think there was still some hope in the back of my mind. But being with Georgia doesn't mean having my mum back. She's gone, and the Georgia I once knew is also gone. It'll never be the same.

"So the other day, I sort of came to the realization that I'd need to let her go for good, which hurt in the moment. But I know it was the right thing to do. I had to finally figure out that I was only hurting myself more by staying with her. Because, in a way, it was all just a game to her. She knew she could use my mum's anniversary as a way to get to me. And I knew that, but I thought again that maybe this time it'd be different. That things could be the same as they were before. But they won't. And in trying to fix things with Georgia, I realized I was hurting you in the process." He takes a deep breath. "I'm sorry."

"Finn." I throw my arms around him, and I don't let go. I hold him tight and let him mourn the loss of his mother, his childhood, and his relationship. Even if I can't relate to him, I know he's hurting.

"Thank you, Livy," Finn finally says, drawing back. "I was thinking about you throughout it all. How you had this change thrown at you, and sure, you were upset in the moment. But I've seen how you've slowly fallen in love with London. And you're right, that change can bring good with it. I don't know what next year will look like, but I know I'll miss having you here."

"Well, about that…"

"What?"

"I think I'm going to make the decision to stay here next year and not go to Boston." Admitting it out loud for the first time feels strange, but there's absolutely no indecision grappling within me. Instead, my words flow out strong and free.

Finn looks at me like I'm a physics problem he can't quite crack. "But all you've been talking about is wanting to go to Boston."

"I know, but now it'd be weird not being in London next year. I don't want to lose all the experiences and friendships I have here. I know I'll fall back into my life at home in the summers, but then I can still have my life in London during the school year. I think that's the best decision for myself."

Finn smiles. "I'm glad, I truly am."

And I am too. Even though we're on a friendship level right now, I don't care. I have my best friend back, things are back to normal, and I'm not losing Finn. There's no need to rush into things if my time in London isn't running out. Sandy would probably say not to rush things, especially with my best friend. I had to trust that everything would work out as it should.

"Hey, let's go to the school pub event tonight and have

fun," I say, remembering the email London City had sent out this morning reminding us of the event. "It'll probably do you good to get out."

He considers it for a moment. "I guess so. Now if you don't mind, I'm going to go back to bed." We stand up in sync, and Finn draws his curtains closed, enveloping us in the darkness. Neither one of us moves, and suddenly, Finn's room feels a thousand times smaller.

"Anyway! Sorry for waking you up way too early on a Saturday," I say and turn toward the door.

Finn follows me and opens the door, the light from the hallway flooding over me like a fresh breath of air.

"It's never a problem to be woken up by you," Finn says as he unties his robe. "I'm so glad we talked."

———

The rest of my Saturday is spent in the library working on an essay for one of my English classes. It's a cloudy day anyway, so I don't mind sitting in the dimly lit library. Shelves of books surround the table I'm working at, and my vanilla latte has sat untouched for too long to still be hot, but I don't care.

I've never been fast at writing essays. After almost four hours, I've only written two pages out of the five required. But this one essay is particularly hard because I want Nicola to know I really put in my best effort. I purposely chose to take another English class with her this semester. I want her to see how far my writing has come and brag about my amazing skills to freshmen in next year's classes.

I take a sip of my cold latte. I'll write one more page, then take a quick lunch break and see how I'm feeling. Bailey texted me an hour ago to see if I wanted to go to some pop-up museum with her and Gabriel and now I'm regretting I said no. If only I could crank out this essay.

"Do you mind if I join you?"

Finn's voice breaks my focus away from my laptop screen. He's standing beside my table, and it's like I fall for him all over again. His curls are no longer a mess, he's wearing my favorite gray sweater, and his aftershave is just strong enough for me to catch a whiff. Judging by the take-out coffee cup in his hand, he hasn't been up for very long.

His hazel eyes stare into mine, waiting for an answer, and I snap out of admiring him.

"Absolutely." I move my textbooks out of the way to make room for him.

He gives a tight smile and takes the chair beside me. "I just woke up," he says.

I glance at the time on my laptop. "It's almost noon."

"It's also a Saturday and I was unexpectedly woken up around eight. Anyway——" Finn sets his backpack down and takes out his notebooks. He carelessly tosses a wax paper bag in front of me. "I was sort of hoping I'd find you here because I picked this up for you on my way."

"No, you didn't." Inside is a warm chocolate chip

cookie from a bakery down the road from Queen Victoria House. "This is exactly what I needed right now."

Finn tries to hold back his smile while taking a pen out of his backpack. "Well, I had to grab a croissant and coffee for breakfast, so don't feel too special."

"You hardly eat breakfast," I say, remembering all the mornings Finn has spent at the caf cutting his food into small pieces.

"Yes, I do. I just rarely have an appetite in the mornings." He takes a long sip of coffee and flips his notebook open. Physics problems crowd his page, making the blue lines of his notebook paper fade into the background.

"Are you working on Nicola's essay?" he asks while he writes out some formula I don't understand.

"I am. It's going to take ages to finish, though."

"You're pretty much guaranteed an A on it, you know that, right?"

"But I want her to be really pleased. You know, like how she bragged to me about how good your writing was."

Finn shakes his head, the corners of his mouth fighting their way up. "That was a completely different class than the one you're in. And our final project was a narrative writing story collection, not an essay comparing works written by dead British authors."

I glance back at my paper. "What did you even write about that was so good?"

Finn swallows. "I wrote about my mum. The whole collection was about her. About what it was like when I was a child, then as a young teenager spending each day after school at hospital with her, then—" Finn writes down another formula. "What it's like now. After."

"I bet that was…" A weight fills my body that crushes all other emotions. "Wow. Heavy stuff."

Finn nods. "She wanted me to share it with my dad and submit it to London City's magazine. She was really proud of my work. But I said no. Some feelings are only meant for you to feel, not the whole world."

He scribbles another problem on his page. "I didn't mean to distract you from your essay."

"You're fine. I don't mean to keep bringing up your mom."

Finn stares at his paper. "It's okay." He tears the page out of his notebook and crumbles it up.

"Are you legit studying for finals, or are you just doing physics for the sake of it?"

He flips his notebook to the next page. "A little bit of both. I do have the final, which will be no problem. It's just kind of relaxing right now." He scribbles another formula off the top of his head.

"Are you and your sister close?" I blurt out. Finn drops his pen, caught off guard. "Sorry. You totally don't have to answer that."

"Not the way it sounds like you are with your siblings. We got on fine enough growing up, but Amy was always the more reasonable one. Whereas I'm the sensitive one apparently, considering I still get emotional about all the little reminders of my mum."

He picks up his pen and starts writing again. "People have different ways of responding to death, I've learned. My sister and my dad are very similar in that regard. That's where they have trouble understanding why I'm still hurting, I reckon."

"I still think you should consider calling your dad," I say. "I really do. I think it could help you."

Finn carelessly lifts a shoulder up to his ear. "He's fine. He's got my sister." He taps my laptop screen. "How's your essay going?"

Nice subject change, Finn.

"Horrible," I say. "I really wanted to finish it today, but I'm literally forcing words out at this point." I scroll back to the top of the page and reread my thesis statement. It's still strong, but my brain has about exhausted all possible ideas about how music is used in Jane Austen's novels.

Finn closes his notebook. "Let's get out of here then. I've missed spending time with my best friend."

My heart sings at his words. I'm his best friend again, and that's all that matters. I put my laptop back in my backpack and follow Finn out of the library. London City University's library sits right in the heart of the city, almost a block away from the British Museum. For some reason, I expect Finn to want to go there only because he's mentioned before how he used to go there so often with his mother. But I'm surprised when Finn walks in the opposite direction, toward the Tube station.

When Emily and Ryan and I would make plans, I

always wanted to know all the details. For my fifteenth birthday, Emily practically begged me to let her host a surprise party. And even though I knew a surprise party was going to happen, I couldn't take not knowing what exactly the surprise would entail. Two weeks before the party, I cornered Ryan after our biology class and made him spill everything Emily had told him about the party. Of course, in true Emily style, she'd planned the most perfect celebration for me. But I was able to relax a lot more going into the party once I knew every detail.

I follow Finn down the stairs to the Tube platform. I don't know where we're going, but for once in my life, I want to be surprised and discover all the tiny details along the way. The Tube car rushes past us, blowing my hair all around me as it comes to a stop. The doors open, and I step in, ready to be whisked off to wherever our final destination might be.

——————

Tower Hill, a station we've gone to all the time for Walking History, is where we make our exit. There's so much in this area which, like the name suggests, includes the Tower of London and Tower Bridge. It's also packed with tourists, but I'm a pro at dodging them now. I walk alongside Finn to the beginning of the bridge.

"It felt fitting to come here and just walk now that the sun's out," Finn says.

"This is one of my favorite places in London," I admit.

The bridge isn't very long, but there's something about walking across the iconic London landmark that feels so surreal. I'm really here, in London, and I know this city now. I was so afraid of the change coming here, but while change is scary, so is staying the same. If I never left Bartonsville, I would've never learned how much I can grow in a new place.

We leisurely walk across the bridge, and I can't stop myself from smiling. It's as if it's just the two of us in this moment. Everyone else around us fades away. We'd walked this bridge countless times together in class, but it always felt like those moments weren't private. But now, even with the crowds of tourists around, this moment feels like it belongs only to us.

My eyes keep straying to Finn. He's staring at me, too, and it feels like everything moves in slow motion as we walk off the bridge toward a small, grassy park. Couples are scattered around, facing the river and city. Dotted here and there are a few lone readers and, of course, plenty of tourists snapping pictures. Finn lies on his back in the grass and spreads his arms out, absorbing the sunshine. I join him and close my eyes. The sun's warmth spreads into my pores, my body soaking it up as if it's never been exposed to the sun before. The minutes pass with a comfortable silence between us. Above us, the gray clouds linger off in the distance, promising an afternoon rain shower. But for now, we'll enjoy this sliver of sun.

Finn pushes himself up into a seated position and brushes the grass off his back. "Did you tell your family you're staying in London for uni?" he asks.

"Not yet. I literally made the decision today." A giddy feeling washes over me. It still doesn't feel real. "But I feel strong in my decision. I think they'll be okay with it. My dad just wants me to be happy. And it's not like I'm moving away forever. I'll still see them over breaks."

"Mm-hmm," Finn says.

"What're your summer plans?" I ask. "Are you staying here?"

"Well, I can't go to my dad's," Finn says. "There's simply not enough room. And I don't really want to be there either. I don't know yet. I can't stay in Queen Victoria House over the summer. I might look into renting a flat here. Or…"

Finn readjusts his glasses, which means he's a bit nervous about what he's going to say. It's so sad that I've watched him so much to know what all his little mannerisms mean.

"What's summer like in Boston?" he says.

I want to jump up and squeal. "It's really nice. It's a lovely city. You'd fit in well. More so than LA, I'd think."

I've never been to LA, but I can hardly picture Finn walking around Malibu wearing summer clothes, surrounded by celebrities. I don't see him lying on the beach or drinking his morning coffee surrounded by palm trees. I can't imagine him being able to relax there when he was trying to escape his reality.

"LA wasn't ever my vibe," Finn says. "It was just the farthest I could get from England and a good internship opportunity. So I made it work for the summer."

"I could see you as some pretentious Harvard summer student. Sitting in some hipster coffee shop for hours on end, doing physics for some new scientific discovery."

"Oh, piss off," Finn says, playfully hitting me. "Although, that'd be pretty cool."

"Nerd."

Finn gives me the British equivalent of the middle finger, the *V* sign. "What time's the pub event tonight?"

"I think Bailey said it's at seven? It's at that pub right down the road from QVH."

Finn glances at his watch. "Right. Are the others coming too?"

I nod. "You know, Bailey and Gabriel have been hanging out a lot. They've gone on a few dates too."

"Congratulations," he deadpans.

I shove his shoulder. "See, I told you they would be good together. And you didn't want to believe me."

"Funny how that happens," Finn says. "People you wouldn't expect to be good together end up as the perfect match. I never would've imagined Bailey and Gabriel together."

We sit together under the London sun, letting the heat warm our faces. This is only the beginning of so much more to come. So many more London afternoons and days spent exploring the city I'd fallen in love with. I can't wait to tell my dad that I've decided to stay.

"You know, Livy," Finn says, breaking our stretch of comfortable silence. "I don't think we're the same people we were at the start of the year. Dealing with all these changes, I think we've been changing too."

I think about the bitter girl I'd been at the start of the academic year. I'd been so sure London wasn't the place for me, that I'd put in my time at London City University, then run back home as soon as I could. But I wasn't that girl anymore. London had taken hold of me, morphed me, and left its mark on me. I'd never be that girl again.

But I'm better now, stronger, and more confident in myself. Without even realizing it, I'd changed and grown slowly, almost like how a caterpillar turns into a butterfly. How beautiful to know that this is only the beginning, that I'll never stop changing and learning and growing.

23

By the time we get back to Queen Victoria House, I don't have much time to get ready for the school pub event. I rarely get dressed up in anything more than jeans and a sweater, but I make more of an effort tonight. I throw open my closet doors and assess the situation before settling on a pale green dress I bought recently when I went shopping with Bailey. I haven't had a chance to wear it and now seems like the perfect opportunity.

I take my hair out of its ponytail and curl it into loose waves. I stand in front of my mirror and actually try to do a full face of makeup that doesn't turn me into a clown.

Finn knocks on my door at 6:45 sharp. I take a deep breath and open the door. It's just him, and he's made a bit more effort tonight too. His curls sit perfectly, and I catch a whiff of his signature cedarwood cologne.

"Wow." His eyes trace all the way down to my feet, then back up. "You look amazing."

Sparks ignite inside me, as if suddenly my entire body has been wired with electricity. It's got to be the soft-pink lipstick I put on. I hardly ever wear lipstick.

I follow Finn down the hall and down the steps of Queen Victoria House. The pub event is at a pub right down the road from the dorm, so the walk is relatively short.

"You've never been here, have you?" says Finn.

"This is my first school pub event, believe it or not." Every month, London City University hosts an event at a local pub that's free and open to all students. The idea is to encourage community and take a break from studying. I'd seen the flyers Gabriel put up each month advertising which pub was hosting, but I'd never gotten around to going.

"You're in for a treat," Finn says. "Ronan usually gets drunk off his arse at these things."

"I haven't forgotten about the last time you and I went out to a pub with everyone else. You were pretty drunk yourself."

"Hey," Finn says. "That's just because Ronan was there. I only go out with him when he drags me away from my work. I don't usually go to these university pub nights. They're always overcrowded. I'm only going tonight because of you."

There's that feeling again, like I'm a shaken soda can that could explode at any second. My heart picks up speed, which only creates more bubbles inside me.

"Just don't succumb to rounds," Finn's saying, oblivious to everything that's happening inside me. "And don't let me fall victim to any of Ronan's peer pressure."

He pushes open the door to the pub, which is reserved just for our school. The dimmed lighting and the wooden walls make the space feel a lot smaller, and Finn shifts closer to me. A school staffer at the entrance hands us a voucher for one free drink, which is their main tactic of getting students to come to these events.

"One," Finn says to me, holding up his finger. "I'm only having one."

We've barely made it into the sea of people before Ronan comes bouncing over to us. He slaps Finn on the back. "What's up, mate? You actually came out tonight."

"Well, you have Olivia to thank for that," Finn says.

Ronan gives me a high five. "Come on." He gestures us over to the bar. "Get your drinks."

"I reckon he's already gone," Finn whispers to me, his breath on my ear sending a shiver all the way down my spine.

We make it over to the bar, and I grip the counter for leverage. Finn hovers beside me as we wait for the bartender. A girl squeezes her way into an open space at the bar, bumping into Finn in the process. Like a domino effect, his chest slams against mine, knocking me off balance. I grab his bicep right as he puts a hand on my shoulder.

"Sorry," he's saying right as the bartender comes over to take our order. I release my grip on his arm and turn to face the bartender before the tingles start to take over my body.

"Cider, please," I hand over my drink voucher and pray the drink will relax me.

"Cheers," Finn says once we receive our pints.

The crowd's gotten bigger since we arrived, and we weave our way over to a corner where Bailey, Gabriel, Hannah, and Ronan are standing. The music vibrates in my veins and rattles my skull. I can see why Finn prefers a regular pub over the university events.

"You guys came," Bailey shouts over the music.

"It's a party now that Finn's here," Ronan says. He leans in to rest his head on Hannah's shoulder.

"It's absolutely not," Finn says. He brings his glass to his lips and takes a long sip.

"Come on, Finn." Ronan nudges his shoulder. "The year's going to be over soon. Have some fun."

"I am having fun," Finn says. "I'm just going to have fun without doing shots."

"Mate," Ronan exclaims, throwing his arms up. "That's the fun part."

"My bloody hangover last time wasn't so fun," Finn deadpans.

"Sure," Ronan says. "Let me know when you change your mind."

As the crowd of students continues to grow, we get pushed more and more into a corner. And even though music's playing at the maximum volume possible, no one's dancing.

"I Want to Hold Your Hand," by The Beatles starts playing. Hannah and Ronan are tangled up in each other's arms, slowly swaying, caught up in their own private moment. Bailey and Gabriel are in full conversation about some band that played a one-night-only show in Sweden, then never released anything again. Finn and I make eye contact. He finishes the last bit of his cider and sets the empty pint on a nearby table. He holds out his hand to me.

"Come with me," Finn says.

I take his hand right as the chorus of the song starts. I don't know where we're going or why he wants to leave, but I don't care. I let my hand mold into his like two pieces of clay. It fits like it's meant to be here in mine.

Once we're out of the pub and into the quiet of the night, Finn leans against the brick building. He lets go of my hand so he can take off his glasses and rub his eyes.

"When you came by my room this morning…" He puts his glasses back on.

So that's what this is about. "Yeah, I'm really sorry again for waking you up. I totally understand if you're tired. We don't have to stay here super late. Or we could go get ice cream somewhere and get away from it all. Or stay. Whatever you—"

"Olivia," Finn cuts me off. "None of that matters."

"What's wrong then?" I hope it's too dark outside for Finn to read the emotions plastered on my face.

"This morning when you came by my room," Finn starts again. He adjusts his glasses even though he just fixed them. "You were right about something, Livy. You said I'm afraid of change, and you were right. I am. I was so afraid to let Georgia go. But I think there's been some good to come out of all of this. Livy, during all our time together, I'm fairly certain I've been falling madly in love with you."

Butterflies swarm in my stomach. If I was already a shaken soda can, Finn just dropped an entire pack of Mentos inside me. I'm full-on exploding now, and there's absolutely no way I can seal the lid. And no way I'd ever want to.

"Wow" is somehow the only word in the entire English language I can manage to pronounce.

"If you don't feel the same way, that's fine," Finn says. "But I just felt the need to be honest with you." He readjusts his glasses again. "I've been denying that I'm in love with you for so long because I was afraid. And I didn't want to lose you at the end of the year. So I kept trying to push my feelings away. But you're the first person I've met here who I can be open with. I feel so safe with you. You're always there for me and you're loving and kind and understanding. My mum would've loved you. And I know she'd want me to be happy."

"You're my best friend here, Finn. I've loved you since right before Christmas break. That night before I left, I should've told you that morning." I explain to Finn my conflicting feelings toward Ryan and why I couldn't confess anything to him in person. "Then, once I realized it was you all along, I got a little worried about the fact that I only had a semester left."

"I think that was holding me back too," he says. "After break, I wanted to be with you so bad. But I was afraid of the heartbreak that would come at the end of the semester. I thought once you were gone, Georgia would be the only one here who could love me. I've been wrong about so much."

The streetlights around us flick on as the darkness begins to take over. A double-decker bus rushes by. So much of this city has become my home. There was so much I'd be leaving behind when the semester ended.

"I think I've been wrong about everything too," I admit.

The streetlight above Finn shines on him like a spotlight. He reaches for his glasses, then drops his hand as if it's on fire.

"I think it's safe to say we've been wrong about a lot this year. But I really hope I'm not wrong about this."

Finn leans forward, cupping his right hand on my cheek and his left on my back. At his touch, my body becomes a streetlight itself, lighting up and radiating electricity all the way down the street. He pulls me closer to him and dips his head, allowing his soft lips to meet mine. It's a quick kiss, but it's like magic. It's like I've ascended into the night sky and become one of the stars themselves. When his lips meet mine, nothing else exists around us.

I want to live in this moment forever. I never want

Finn's lips to leave mine. When he pulls away, I grab his hand.

"Finn," I say. "I can promise you, you're definitely not wrong about that."

He kisses me again, and it all feels so right. We walk back into the pub and find that Hannah, Ronan, Bailey, and Gabriel have secured a table and are busy playing some card game. Ronan managed to get another pint in the meantime.

"Where'd you guys go?" Bailey asks. "We looked over, and you were gone."

Finn and I lock eyes. "We just needed to get some air for a minute," Finn says. "Bit stuffy in here." The secret exists between us, unknown to the rest of the world.

Under the table, Finn takes my hand. His thumb sits on top, rubbing gentle circles. I hope he never stops. I want to freeze this moment in time. When I get home to Bartonsville for the summer, I want to paint Finn's hand in mine so I can have it with me even when I don't have him.

"You're not just staying in London for me, are you?" he whispers.

I shake my head. "It'd be weird if I didn't come back," I say. "There's too much here that I'd be leaving behind." Wine nights with Bailey and Hannah. Ronan's energy every single day. Chats with Gabriel. Living in a city I'd fallen in love with. It was all a part of me now.

"And that's the game," Ronan shouts, pumping his fist

in the air to celebrate his victory. Hannah leans over and kisses his cheek.

"Proud of you, babe," she says.

Ronan collects the cards and returns them to their case. Finn nudges my shoulder.

"You should tell them," he whispers. "It's a great excuse for them to celebrate some more." He nods his head in Ronan's direction. "*Especially* him."

So I do. Finn squeezes my hand as I get the group's attention and break my exciting news to them.

"Olivia, that's so exciting," Bailey says. "You've made the best choice, trust me. London City is so much better than Boston Southeast."

"I'm really excited," I say, and I mean it with every ounce of my being. It's a big decision to make, but I'm proud of myself for doing what feels best for me.

"I knew you'd come around to London," Gabriel says.

"Cheers to that," Ronan says, and he clinks glasses with Hannah. Finn raises his eyebrows in an *I told you so* manner. "I'm going to get some shots. Shots for everyone?"

Hannah, Bailey, and Gabriel cheer, ready for any reason to celebrate.

"Can we go home?" Finn whispers to me. "I don't want to wait any longer to be alone with you." He glances at our friends. "Selfishly, I don't really want to share right now."

I squeeze his hand as I lean my head onto his shoulder. I don't want to wait any longer, either. I just want Finn all alone, all mine, forever.

"Let's go home," I say. It's the first time I've said *home* and meant Queen Victoria House and not Massachusetts. It feels good and right.

On our walk back, Finn's hand never leaves mine. He lets go only to fumble in his pocket for his key to the building. We walk down the hall to my dorm room, and then it's my turn to find my key.

"Can I come by in about ten minutes?" Finn says. "If that's alright? We can have a redo on our Hyde Park night."

"That's perfect," I say, then pull Finn in for one more kiss. He holds my hand until our arms stretch apart and he has to let go in order to get to his door.

"I'll see you soon," he says.

I walk into my room, where Finn's tea towel he'd given me for Christmas seems to add a touch of hope. This place used to be so bland and empty, but next year, I'll have more. Next year, Finn and I will browse vintage stores for cool pieces or old magazines. He'll be here on my first day back, ready to help me hang some decorations in the places I can't reach. Then we'll spend the evening together without fear of our time ever running out.

In the silence of my room, the seconds stretch on and on as I wait for Finn. My foot's been tapping softly against my hardwood floor. If Emily were here, she'd know every detail about Finn. It's strange that

I've navigated all these feelings without her by my side.

I calculate the time back in Boston. It's late afternoon, so Emily's probably around. But we haven't talked since Christmas break and when everything went down with Ryan and Maddie. But if I've learned anything, losing Finn for that short period of time was awful. I don't want to lose Emily or Ryan. I pick up my phone and decide to give her a call, even if it's out of the blue.

"Hey, Olivia," Emily answers after a few rings. "It's been a while."

"I know, and I'm really sorry. Genuinely, really sorry. I've learned a lot about being away and change. You guys did nothing wrong. It was all me. Of course you and Ryan would have new friendships, and I was just being jealous all along," I say.

She's quiet for a bit. "I've missed you, Olivia. And I'm sorry, too, for pushing you away when life got busy. I want to see you when you come home for the summer. Just us. I want it to be just like old times."

"Absolutely," I say. I know I can still have my friendship with Emily. It might not ever be exactly the same or under the circumstances I thought, but we would always have each other. "But about that…"

"What?" Emily says. "Don't tell me you aren't coming home now."

"Well, sort of. I'll be home for the summer, but I've made the decision to complete the rest of college over here in London. You were right from the very beginning.

This is such a great opportunity, and I'd be crazy to pass it up."

I can almost imagine Emily's smile filling her face even from miles away. If I was there, she'd probably jump up and down and give me a hug. This is what she would want me to do. She was always trying to push me out of my comfort zone and be more adventurous.

"Liv, I'm so proud of you," she says. "One hundred percent serious. And I can't wait to spend all summer with you."

"Well, now you have an excuse to visit London for spring break next year *and* have a free place to stay!" Second-years had the option to live in Queen Victoria House or get a shared flat. Bailey had already been discussing the logistics of everyone getting a flat together. I couldn't wait to discuss details with her later.

"I'm going to start looking for flights right now," Emily says.

"One more thing. I might be seeing someone over here."

I'm positive all of Boston and London can hear Emily's scream. "What! No way! Who? I need all the details."

I fill Emily in on everything about Finn from the day we met all the way until now. My heart sings again, recounting all the little details of our story.

We talk a bit more about how Ryan's doing and how Emily's semester is going. I've learned now that this change was for a reason and that everything will be okay when I go home. I'll still have Emily and Ryan as friends. And they'll still want to see me and spend time with me too.

I hang up and toss my phone on the bed right as Finn knocks at my door. Perfect timing.

"Hi," I say. Finn's standing there in my favorite gray sweatpants paired with a black sweater. He's clutching a paperback novel.

"Hi," he says, and his face melts into a smile.

I take his hand and lead him into my room. "Make yourself comfortable," I say. "For real this time."

Finn puts his navy slippers by my door, revealing tan socks dotted with chess pieces.

"Nice socks."

"Hey now," Finn says. "Chess is cool."

He lifts his sweater over his head, exposing his abs for a second. But his sliver of skin is quickly covered by his faded white band T-shirt.

"I won't take anything else off," Finn says, smiling. He totally caught me staring.

"I don't mind if you do," I find myself saying. My face heats like the desert in the summer.

"I'm going to shower," I say before Finn can say anything. "I'll be right back."

———

When I come back to my room, Finn has already made

himself comfortable in my bed. He's so engulfed in some book he doesn't even hear me come in.

And his shirt's off.

My duvet is pulled up to his chest, but his bare shoulders peak above. And his arms. His long, toned arms. I never knew Finn worked out. He never mentioned it. But he must. Maybe he has some secret gym membership I've never known about.

"Always doing something academic," I say as I gather my hair into a high ponytail.

He places the book on the desk behind my bed and scoots over for me to squeeze in next to him. "Reading before bed is relaxing. It helps to clear your mind."

I laugh. "Only you would say that."

He kisses me again, soft and gentle like before. I rest my head on his shoulder.

"What's this?" I say, running my fingers along a small tattoo just below his right collarbone. HCA. "I didn't know you had a tattoo."

"My mum," he says. "It's her initials."

I trace my finger over the letters. "Did it hurt?"

He shakes his head. "I already felt so numb when I went in for the appointment. It was like the world was simply existing around me. If anything, the pain from the tattoo gun felt good in the moment. It made me feel something. It made me feel alive."

"Finn," I wrap my arm around him. "I hope you never hurt like that again. I wish I could take all the pain you've ever felt away from you."

My arm rises and falls with Finn's breathing. "I'm so lucky to have you," he finally says. "So, so lucky to have you, my Olivia."

My Olivia. I melt into a puddle right there. "Finn," I say. "My handsome, thoughtful Finn. I'm so lucky too."

He takes off his glasses and tugs the switch on my lamp. He pulls me closer to him and lets his arm rest on my back. "Goodnight, Livy," he whispers into my ear.

In the darkness, my head falls against Finn's chest, and his heartbeat echoes in my ear like music. His arm stays wrapped around me all night, and we squeeze together to share my twin bed. We become closer and closer until two become one as we drift off into sleep.

24

Sunshine fills my room at six in the morning, and
I'm wide awake. I can't help it; I've always been an
early riser. Beside me, Finn doesn't stir. A soft snore
echoes from his nose. Everything about him is beautiful.
I can't believe this is real life right now. His eyes are
shut, making even his eyelashes seem delicate and
perfect.

I'm careful to lift his arm and place it on my pillow as
I get out of bed. I tiptoe through my tiny dorm room as
careful as a ballerina, grabbing my stuff to wash my face
and change in the water closet.

When I come back to my room, I open the door very,
very slowly so it doesn't creak, then sit at my desk. I
should get some more work done on my paper. I dig
around through my backpack for a pen and take out my
laptop.

Finn shifts in bed. "God damn it, Livy, why are you

up so early?" he says, his voice heavy with sleep. He rubs his eyes and loudly groans.

"I'm just working on my paper. You can go back to sleep."

Finn tugs the duvet over his head. "Ugh, I am."

By nine, I'm starving and ready for breakfast. Finn's snoring, louder this time, so I make a quick run to the caf. I take a blueberry scone and a coffee to go for Finn.

An hour and a half later, I'm finished with my paper, and Finn finally starts to stir. He yawns and sits up.

"About time," I say.

"Piss off," Finn mumbles and reaches for his glasses.

"Good morning to you too. I brought you back some breakfast."

"God, Livy, you're the best." Finn stretches his arms and pushes back my duvet. "I'm going to have a shower and eat, then I'll be back."

I busy myself doing a thirty-minute online yoga practice, but once it's over, Finn isn't back. He doesn't strike me as someone who'd take a long shower, but it'd make sense with him always running late for breakfast. I decide to browse some online shops and see if there are any new spring outfits I want to order. After I've filled my online cart to the brim, then made my final selections and checked out, there's still no sign of Finn. No texts or missed calls from him either.

It's getting close to an hour now, and I'm ready to get on with my day. I wait another minute, then go down to Finn's room. I knock once.

Finn opens the door. His curls are damp and he's changed into a fresh T-shirt and jeans. "I'm sorry," he says.

He's wide awake now, but his face offers no emotion. "Is everything okay?" I ask.

"I'm fine," he states and runs his fingers through his curls. He takes a sharp inhale. "I just called my dad."

"Finn." I throw my arms around him. I can't believe it. Finn lets me into his room and we both sit on his black duvet.

"It just feels sort of weird, you know?" Finn says. "To call someone up who you barely talk to?"

"And? What'd you say? What did he say?"

"I apologized. I told him I was sorry for blowing him off after my mum died and for being all moody every time I went home to Liverpool. And he apologized, too, for not always being there for me when I was struggling. It was actually a rather healthy conversation," Finn says. "It was strange at first, but I feel much better about things now, I think."

I take Finn's hand in mine. "I'm so glad you did that," I say. "I'm really, really proud of you."

"It was all because of you, or I never would've," Finn says. "All that stuff you said about me being afraid of change and letting things go. Deep inside, I didn't want to let go of the fact that my mum was gone." He sniffles and takes his glasses off to rub his eyes. I feel like my heart is glass, shattering into millions of pieces. I wish I could absorb all his pain so he'd never hurt again.

"But she's gone, and my dad's all I've got right now." He straightens up, pulls himself together. "All along, he's been there to support me and pay for uni, and I've just been all moody toward him. Anyways, my dad really wants me to spend the summer in Liverpool with him."

"Are you going to?"

Finn shrugs. "The houseboat is still a tad too small for two people, in my opinion. So I think I'm going to divide up my time. Maybe spend a few weeks in Germany with my sister here and there."

Sunlight seeps into Finn's dark dorm room. It was so hard to imagine that there was once a time I didn't want to be in London. In two weeks, I'd be back in Massachusetts for the summer. I squeeze Finn's hand.

"Let's go enjoy the day while the sun's shining," I say. "And enjoy the time we still have together."

———

After our Tube journey, Finn and I make our way up to Primrose Hill. The spring breeze blows my hair and makes my white floral dress flow around me. Finn has a yellow blanket tucked under his arm. When we find a good spot, he spreads it out on top of the hill. We join the dots of couples and friends crowding the hill, enjoying the warm day. A few months ago, I was like the tourists, snapping pictures, but today, I'm a local passing my time in one of my favorite places in London.

A group of six friends sit on the blanket nearest us. I

listen in on their conversation and realize how much I'll miss every part of this city. Beyond our post on the hill, London's skyline stands in full view. Not a single cloud fills the sky, and every building stands to be admired. Even the trees in the park are more vibrant now that their spring leaves have come back.

"I'm glad everything turned out the way it did," Finn says.

I lay my head in his lap and he runs his fingers through my hair. "Me too," I say. "What I thought was the worst thing that could've happened to me turned out to be the best thing ever."

Finn dips his head down and kisses me. "Maybe you've proved that not all change is bad. You're the best change that's ever happened to me."

I push Finn down so our heads are lying side by side and kiss him again.

"Livy," Finn says. "We're one of those couples now."

"Huh?"

"Remember?" Finn asks. "That time we came to the park with everyone else, and we were making fun of those couples making out on their blankets? We're one of them now."

I laugh. "I don't care. I love you way too much to care what anyone thinks."

A smile creeps across Finn's face. "I love you too, Livy."

EPILOGUE

Heathrow Airport is like a bustling city with everyone coming and going. A man in a suit dashes between Finn and me, dragging a black suitcase behind him. This is it, the day I'd been counting down to since the start of school. In a little over seven hours, I'd be back in Boston, but I'm feeling the opposite of what I thought I'd feel at the start of the year.

"Call me as soon as you get in," Finn says. "I don't care what the time difference is. Getting woken up to hear your voice is absolutely worth it."

"And tell me when you get back to Liverpool," I say.

Finn pulls me in for a hug. "We'll talk every day," he promises. "And I'll see you in a month."

Finn agreed to spend June in Liverpool with his dad and half of July in Germany with his sister. He found a good flight deal to Boston at the beginning of July, so we'll get to spend two weeks together, and he'll get to meet my family and friends. I'll be returning to London mid-August and will travel around with Finn before classes start back up.

I smile and try to hold back tears. "I'll miss you so, so much."

Finn kisses my forehead. "I'll miss you too, but your family and friends need you. And you need them too. It'll be no time until I'm there. Then it'll practically be time for us to explore Paris, then back to the grind. We're going to be okay," he says. "I believe in us, Livy."

And it's that bit of reassurance I needed. We'll be okay. Finn believes in us. I have a home now in Massachusetts and London. And I wouldn't want to have it any other way.

"I'll see you real soon," I say.

One more long kiss. I'll miss his touch and seeing him every day, but Finn's right. My family needs me, and so do my friends. I drag my big suitcase behind me as I head down to check my bag. I turn back and wave one final goodbye. But this isn't goodbye forever. This isn't the end. It's just the beginning of our adventure.

ACKNOWLEDGMENTS

Writing a book is a very solidarity activity. There's only one writer, after all. But thankfully, I put together the most supportive team. This book couldn't have been possible without the behind-the-scenes help I had.

First, thank you to my amazing editor, Sarah McGuire. I'm so glad I found you. Your edits helped me polish my story and make it the best it could be. I knew my drafts were in good hands. Thank you for supporting me through this process and for all our chats about writing in general.

Darius Kelly, thank you for working with me to bring my cover vision to life. I appreciate all the time you spent working on it and making my dreams come true.

Thank you to Maryssa Gordon for proofreading my work and making sure everything was ready for publication.

I'm lucky to have friends who are willing to dedicate time to reading a draft of a book that needs feedback. Alex Soltys, you're not afraid to be honest about what's working in my writing and what's not, and that's absolutely the kind of feedback I needed. Matthew Balcewicz, thank you for loving and believing in Olivia and Finn.

To my brother, Josh. This story wouldn't have even become an actual book without your help. From the very beginning, you believed in me and supported me. Even though you aren't a romance genre fan or a reader, you still read my very first draft and gave me detailed feedback. And through the rest of my drafts, you were there for me in so many ways. I'm so thankful for you.

To all of my friends who offered encouragement along the way— thank you. I've been in my writing cave and focused on this book for so long. Thanks for listening to me when I went off on tangents about "the book."

And of course, to my parents. You're always my biggest supporters. I don't think there are enough words to express my thanks.

Lastly, to every single person who reads my book. It means the world to me that you took the time to read this story that I've poured my soul into. Thank you, thank you, thank you.

ABOUT THE AUTHOR

Samantha Kramer is an author from Charleston, South Carolina. She loves a good romance story, the city of London, and anything crafty/creative. Find her on social media @samanthakramerwrites

www.ingramcontent.com/pod-product-compliance
Lightning Source LLC
Chambersburg PA
CBHW011321310726
48973CB00011B/3004